FIGHT IN THE MOUNTAINS

FIGHT
IN
THE
MOUNTAINS

Christian Bernhardsen

TRANSLATED FROM
THE DANISH
BY FRANEY SINDING

HARCOURT, BRACE & WORLD, INC.
NEW YORK

1

CHRIS had been sitting on a branch of the oak overhanging the sloping hillside for almost two hours when the explosions began. They echoed through the mountains like thunder. Then the flames shot up into the sky, casting an evil glare over the blacked-out town.

Chris clenched his fists, elated.

The fire grew fiercer. The stuttering sound of machine-gun fire tore into the stillness, but it did not frighten the boy in the tree. Perhaps it was Bent firing that gun. He knew his brother was out there somewhere. Almost always when Bent left home in the evening, there were explosions later, and each time Chris was at his lookout post in the tree.

Now the oil tanks on the distant promontory, which stuck out into the ocean beyond the town, were ablaze. They made an enormous bonfire, a marvelous spectacle! Yet something unexpected must have happened. The exchange of gunfire, which normally was scattered, grew more intense and went on for long minutes.

The thought that Bent could get hurt didn't even occur to

5

Chris. Bent was invulnerable. Bent was the only person left whom he could trust.

The sea around the promontory seemed to be on fire, too, as the burning oil spread. The whole promontory and the pine forest beyond it were in flames. To the boy in the tree, it looked as if the horizon itself was burning.

The explosions continued, and after each of them a column of flames shot up nearby as high as the mountains. The shooting petered out slowly. Chris could hear the piercing wail of the sirens as the fire engines started from the town.

But no one would be able to quell the fire that Bent had started, even if they tried—and the firemen would not! They would roll out their hoses, connect the foam extinguishers, and then they would light a cigarette rolled out of newspaper with tobacco they had grown in their own yards. The fire on the promontory was not their fire.

Chris chuckled. He could imagine how the Nazis on the promontory would be darting about in their green uniforms, screaming and shouting. They had fired their machine guns at an unseen enemy—at Bent and his friends. The promontory would burn for days to come, and then there would be new explosions and new fires.

One day the Nazis would stand with their faces to the wall and their arms above their heads—the way he had done, the way Bent had done, the way all the others now gone had done. He longed to see them defeated and shamed.

For some time Chris sat watching the blazing fire give the mountains threatening shapes. Then he climbed along the thick branch toward the balcony. Beyond was his room. He had to be there when Bent came home. Bent must not know that he stayed awake to watch.

He was just about to swing himself over the balustrade when the black cars came. They came quite slowly, almost gliding.

There were two of them. They stopped outside the garden gate, and men swarmed out of them. Some wore black leather coats and had one hand thrust deep into a pocket. Some were soldiers, ready with their machine guns. No orders were given. The soldiers kicked open the gate and surrounded the house. The men in black coats walked toward the front door. One of them hammered on it.

"Open up! It's the police!" When no one answered, he roared, "Gestapo!"

The black-coated men had drawn their guns, and one of them put his shoulder to the door; but the door was unlocked. They rushed in, shooting. They need not have bothered. The house was empty.

Chris sat astride the branch, trembling. On the gravel path just below him, a soldier was on guard. There were soldiers everywhere, and in the house were the men in black. Chris could follow their movements from room to room by the faint chinks of light that flickered through the blackout curtains.

They weren't going to get him. They weren't going to get Bent, either. They weren't going to get anyone else in that house.

One of the men in black leather came out again. He gave quick orders; the cars drove off, and the soldiers were hidden in the darkness. All lights in the house went out.

Chris edged himself back along the branch. He was as nimble as a squirrel. Even in the dark he knew every twig. Once out in his tree house, he sat thinking.

The branches of the tree were so thick that no one from the house could see him. Beneath the tree, the hillside sloped toward the railroad tracks and the gaping darkness of the tunnel.

Up here he had built his tree house. At first he had used old boards and straw and whatever else he could find. He could look out over the city and dream of adventure. He had made up several stories. The first stories had been quite beautiful, but they were beautiful no more.

It all began on that day two years ago. He had been very happy with a new pair of skates he had received for his fourteenth birthday, and when he came home from trying them out on the ice, the street was full of cars and soldiers.

He was ready to turn back. His friends in school had had plenty of stories to tell, but he had not believed them. True, there were soldiers in uniform with guns and helmets; they had arrived one morning and had completely changed the quiet rhythm of the little town. Blackout curtains were put on all windows, food was rationed, and there was a curfew after dark. So naturally he had been aware that there was a war, but nevertheless, in some strange way, it did not really concern him.

He had read a lot about wars in his history books, but they told mainly about dates. He had read a lot about heroism in the history books, too.

There he stood on the street and was terribly afraid, and a woman he had never seen before shrilled hysterically, "He's one of them!"

8

After that all was confusion. There wasn't time to run.

A soldier rammed the butt of his rifle hard into his back, so that he fell and dropped his skates. An officer slapped the soldier across the face with his gloves and ordered him to pick up the skates. The woman who had a strange scar over her left eye was herded into a car.

Then Chris stood facing the officer, alone.

"Sorry," said the German. "We do not wage war on children." He stared as coldly at Chris as he had at the soldier and the woman.

He spoke perfect Norwegian. "Let's go."

Chris followed him silently—through the garden gate, over the gravel path, up the stairs, and in through the door. He hurried because he was sure something terrible had happened.

"Easy boy," said the officer. "We'll get there soon enough." Much later Chris realized that his remark might have been kindly meant.

His father was lying in the library—the dark dining room with the many books that they called the library. His father was dead. Most of his head had been shot off. In his hand he held a gun. Two Germans lay dead in a corner of the room. Bent stood with his face thrust against a bookshelf. If it hadn't been for the machine gun a soldier was pressing into his back, it might have been a comical sight—Bent with his nose shoved against books by Schiller.

There were several other people in the room, men in black leather coats.

"Well, young man," said the officer. His eyes were like ice. "What can you tell us?"

Chris could tell them nothing.

9

The officer went on, "I suppose you didn't know that your father, the connoisseur of German culture in this ridiculous town, conspired against us? I suppose you did not know that your father published illegal newspapers with distorted items of news? I suppose you did not know that your father, a would-be guiding influence on the young, encouraged acts of sabotage? Didn't you know, boy? Answer!"

Chris had no answer.

The heap on the carpet was no concern of his. It was something that once had been his father. Up against the wall stood Bent, and Bent was alive.

"I'm here, Bent," he said quietly. And his brother Bent nodded slightly.

"Look at your father instead," spat the officer. "He killed two of my men."

But Chris sickened at the sight and turned away. His father was ugly in death. Some day they would pay for this.

"Who comes to this house?" raged the officer, stamping his foot furiously.

"I don't know," said Chris, and shrugged his shoulders.

He did not know. That was the truth. He wished he could lie. He hated them for killing his father, but he had no lies to tell. He wanted to cry, but he could not cry, even though they started beating him.

Now the men in black were here after Bent again. They had come in vain. He would see to it that they left empty-handed. He knew which way Bent would return from the night's raid, and he would be there to intercept him.

He would have a long wait, but he was comfortable in his tree house overhanging the slope. He had had this hideout in the tree ever since he was a little boy. Sometimes he would sit all day in the great oak and look out over the town and harbor and watch the trains skim over the short stretch of rail between the two tunnels. One of the tunnels led almost into the central railroad station. Bent generally used that for his return route. The other tunnel went under the hill and ended at the edge of town, where large blocks of apartment buildings intermingled with farms. The mountains rose directly and steeply from the fields. Chris never liked going there, not even in the winter when there was snow on the ground. The area was neither town nor country.

It was after an air raid during which shrapnel from the ack-ack guns smashed the tiles over the bay window in his room that he had made his hideout in the tree into a regular tree house. He had put on a tin roof and covered it with sod and had filled the cracks and chinks in the walls. After that he sat there when the bombers came roaring in over the town and felt a rush of joy each time the bombs exploded. He sat there when Bent was away.

Bent was two years older than he and was in his last year at high school.

It had been a bad time after their father's death. They had both been taken into the Gestapo headquarters for questioning. They had not been allowed to sit beside each other. Chris had been shown into a cell just large enough to hold a cot. At least three times a day he had been taken out for questioning. Sometimes it was the officer with the cold eyes who questioned, sometimes it was one of the men in black. The woman with the scar had been there as interpreter.

Each time it was the same question: "Who came to the house to see your father?"

And each time the answer was: "I don't know."

11

Sometimes the questioning went on for hours, but they stopped beating him.

After eight days they gave him the keys to the house and turned him loose.

In a way, he never wanted to see the house again after what had happened inside, but nevertheless he felt oddly happy as he put the key in the lock. This was where he belonged.

The blood-stained carpet was still there in the dining room. One of the very first things he did was to haul it out into the garden, pour gasoline over it, and burn it.

He carefully swept the ashes together and buried them under the big tree. The Nazis had grinned when he had asked them where his father was buried.

"We do not bury swine," said one of the men in black. "We feed them to the swine."

The words rang in his ears as he laid the sod over the ashes. Then he began to clean up.

Everything in the house was a shambles. The books were pulled off the shelves, and the pages were torn. Every cupboard and drawer had been broken into; there was paper everywhere. Maybe he would have given up if the neighbors hadn't come to help. He had his meals with them, but he always slept in the house. Bent should not find it empty when he returned.

Some days later Bent appeared suddenly. He never spoke about his time at Gestapo headquarters, but his face was swollen, and he had one arm in a sling.

"I told them nothing," he said in reply to Chris's silent question.

12

"But you knew?"

"Of course!"

Chris asked no more questions. He knew they would not be answered. Bent put his good arm tenderly around his brother's shoulders. "War is not for children," he said, and his eyes were full of sadness. "But we'll manage well enough."

Chris stiffened defiantly. That's what the officer had said! He caught himself wishing that the war would last long enough so that he could show them.

So the routine of everyday life began once more in the house on the hillside. Still, nothing was the way it had been before. The neighbors were helpful, and the school where their father had taught took care of their finances. They lacked nothing. Yet their relationship had changed. They were no longer two boys nearly the same age, but instead an adult and a child.

Chris felt let down when Bent began staying away in the evenings. It wasn't until he understood the connection between Bent's absences and the explosions and fires that he could look upon Bent as a friend again. Just knowing this made him feel as if he were helping. This evening the part he was playing was at last real. As he slowly let himself down out of the tree, he felt that he was now one of the underground. He was no longer a boy.

He met Bent at the mouth of the tunnel. His brother leaned heavily against the side and would have pitched forward headlong if Chris hadn't caught him. In the dim light Chris could see that one-half of his face was covered with clotted blood.

13

"What happened to you, Bent?" he whispered.

His brother looked at him with glazed eyes. "What are you doing here?"

"I'm here, Bent, because the Gestapo have surrounded the house. They are after you."

"And you," said Bent with a heavy sigh. "This time neither of us will get away."

"Nonsense!"

The firm sound of his own voice surprised Chris. Bent stared at him. Then he rapped his head as if to knock out the pain.

"Of course," he said. "We just have to get through the next tunnel; then Tom will take care of the rest."

"Who's Tom?"

"Don't ask questions—give me your arm."

Chris put his arm around his brother for support, intensely proud that he now was almost as tall as Bent.

They staggered along the railroad ties toward the tunnel under the hill.

"What happened?" Chris repeated.

"Everything went wrong."

"But the entire promontory is on fire."

"Yes, the promontory is burning, but the others will never come back. Those damned Nazis knew we were coming, but they must have gotten their signals mixed, too. Otherwise, we couldn't have carried out our plan. Oil enough for a hundred submarine missions is burning now. Oil for a hundred submarine missions! That's something they'll feel! They managed to cut us off, though. I was the only one to get through."

14

They had almost reached the second tunnel when an air raid began. The scream of sirens cut through the night, and immediately searchlights began fanning the skies. They could hear the muffled roar of the antiaircraft guns down along the coast and the deep, monotonous drone of planes steadily coming closer.

Bent grabbed Chris.

"They're here!" he exulted.

"Let's get out of here."

Half laughing, half stumbling, they hurried into the tunnel under the hill.

2

THE tunnel was short. It took the train only a minute to go through. They could not be safer anywhere else, but they had to hurry. They had to reach the other side before the air raid was over, while people were all in shelters. This was their only chance. It was difficult to follow the tracks. They stumbled along, fell, picked themselves up, and hurried on.

Suddenly they were out in the open.

The bombers were coming over in waves. Fire from the ack-ack guns filled the sky like gigantic crackling fireworks. Tracer bullets showered the town like confetti. The fields were bared by the stark white light each time a flare exploded. The apartment buildings looked like ugly barracks in the glare.

The submarine base was being bombed.

"Now people are dying," thought Chris, but somehow it didn't bother him, even though he realized that many of his own people were dying, too.

In the light of the huge fire, he could see how the heavy bombers made straight for their target one by one. Then they gained altitude and disappeared over the mountains. Chris thought it was a wonderful sight, and he said so. But Bent was in low spirits again, and he answered angrily, "The fools came too late."

They ran across the fields, along country paths, through hedges and gardens. Bent was still irritable, but he had forgotten his wound. All that mattered now was getting through.

Chris wondered at his brother's change of mood, but he dared not ask about it. There was no time. As soon as the air raid was over, people would stream out of houses and shelters. German vehicles would patrol the roads again.

Bent did not stop till they reached the foot of the mountain. His head wound was open again, and blood was running down his face.

"Here we are," he said out of breath. They had not met a soul. "We must be careful now," he added.

The bombers had stopped coming, the searchlights were turned off, and only occasional shots from the ack-ack guns could be heard. Then the all clear sounded. A terrible fire was burning near the harbor, where the submarine base lay. It couldn't be the base itself burning, for that was all steel and concrete. The town was on fire.

Bent leaned tiredly against the gatepost and said once again, "Everything went wrong."

They stood by a small house on the edge of the forest. They stood there for a long time, and Chris had a feeling that Bent was afraid. It began to snow, and soon the fire in the town could be seen only as a faint red glow.

The house was dark and silent. Was that why Bent was

17

afraid? Chris was afraid, too. Reluctantly he said, "You said that we were here . . . now!"

"Yes, Tom lives here," Bent replied.

"Who's Tom?"

"Possibly a traitor."

"Bent!" Chris stepped up to his brother. "Your head!" The wound was bleeding fast.

Bent let go of the gatepost, lurched a little, and then stood erect in front of Chris.

"Yes, I need help," he said. "But first I must find out for certain."

He opened his windbreaker with difficulty. In a holster under his left arm, he had a pistol. He drew it and released the safety catch. Then he said, "Wait here, and if you hear shots, run! Remember now, run!" He opened the gate and walked slowly up to the house.

Only hours ago Chris had been a schoolboy. He had done his homework, even his German, and had carefully considered what lessons he could skip—he needed time to sit in the tree house.

All that schoolwork—compositions, writing, and even gym—didn't exist any more.

He followed his brother quietly.

Bent stopped unsteadily in front of the door. He staggered but got hold of the banister and dragged himself up the steps.

"Are you there, Tom?" he shouted.

There was no answer.

"Tom," he repeated desperately, "open up!"

18

But the house was as silent as the mountain towering above it.

"Tom!"

It was a cry of distress, but it was also a cry of warning. Bent raised his pistol and fired blindly.

Then a series of shots came from within, splintering the door. Bent fell, but he had not been hit. When the door was kicked open, from inside, he was pushed down the steps and lay face down on the ground.

Chris was numb with fear. He wanted to run, but he couldn't. In the light from the open door, he could see the snow under Bent's head turn sickeningly red. A man appeared on the top step. His face was hard, and he was holding a machine gun. He lowered the barrel toward Bent's head before he rolled Bent over on his back with one foot.

At this Chris jumped him. The man dropped the machine gun in the powdery snow, and it slipped away out of reach. Chris was not full-grown, and a flashing blow to the jaw sent him sprawling. Barely conscious, he heard a scared, "Good God, it's Bent!"

"And I am his brother."

Chris picked himself up. He was confused.

"Are you Tom?" he asked.

"Yes, I'm Tom all right."

The man in the house at the edge of the forest had retrieved his machine gun, and he looked questioningly at Chris.

"What's this fuss supposed to mean?"

"I don't know," answered Chris, "but Bent is hurt."

"Yes, I can see that."

Together they carried him in and laid him on a sofa. Tom began gently rinsing Bent's wound. Suddenly Chris recognized him. He was older than Bent, maybe twenty-five years old, and a well-known skier. Chris had admired him greatly. He looked at him uncertainly.

"What are you gaping at, boy? Your brother has scraped his face and lost a little blood, but otherwise he is all right."

"Are you a traitor?"

Tom was just about to hit Chris when Bent opened his eyes and sat up suddenly.

"Tom, was it you?" he said in a strangely loud voice.

"Shut up, you fool. You started shooting and pretty nearly got me!"

Tom held out a burned spot on his sweater.

"This is how close you got. Good thing you fell over before I fired."

Bent dropped back onto the pillow.

"Why didn't you come?" he said.

"I came"—Tom's eyes were steady, and his voice was calm—"but it was all over."

"The planes came after it was all over, too." Bent smashed one hand into the wall. "Something is terribly wrong."

"We must talk about that later."

Tom went out into the kitchen and poured out two generous shots of gin. He gave one to Bent, and they drank.

"Is it from over there?" asked Bent.

"You bet," answered Tom.

20

Chris envied them—not the drinking, but their fellow-ship.

Bent's wound was still bleeding. Tom refilled the glasses and began to tie on a bandage. He was not very skilled at it, and the bandage ended up looking like a bulky turban.

Bent felt revived and finally said to Chris, "Good thing you came along."

Chris flushed with pleasure, but Tom had no time for sentiment.

"Tell me what happened," he said shortly. "We haven't much time."

And Bent began.

"There should have been six of us. Five of us were to take care of two oil tanks each, and the sixth was to stand guard by the boat. But you didn't come. We waited five minutes by the dock in the bay before we rowed away. According to the plan we all had received, the bombardment was to begin at nine-thirty. At nine-thirty-five, the fake attack on the guards was to be launched from land, and at nine-forty we were to go ashore on the promontory.

"The planes were supposed to come at ten-thirty." Tom's face was white with anger. "That was what I suggested to London and London accepted. It said ten-thirty on my final orders as well."

"Who gave you the order?"

"Paul, who else!"

"How did you get it?"

"In a letter put in the mailbox, as usual."

"And how did you send your OK to Paul?"

"As always: General Delivery at the main post office—to Paul Jensen."

"Who is Paul Jensen?"

Tom looked doubtfully at Bent. He said, "Do you know?"

Chris could see that only his brother's weakness kept him from hurling himself at the other man.

"You know darned well," he answered, "that I don't know who Paul is. Nobody knows. It could be you."

"Or you!"

"Yes, both of us survived."

"We have to clear this up before we go on," said Bent dispiritedly.

"With pleasure." Tom shrugged his shoulders with seeming indifference, but Chris noticed that he glanced at the machine gun on the table.

Bent continued. "Then the truth is that you, as the radio operator for the group, were ordered by Paul to wire London, suggesting we blow up the oil tanks—a mission that included attacks from land and from the sea—and that an air bombardment be started a little before to distract the enemy. Two birds with one stone. What's more, it is certain that the plan was Ok'd and that you sent it on to Paul as usual."

Tom nodded. "That's just the way it happened."

"But the message that reached our groups timed the mission an hour ahead."

Tom nodded once more.

"And the result was that we got there too early, and the planes got there too late!"

Tom still said nothing, and Bent literally hurled the words at him. "Why don't you say something!"

"I'm just thinking," answered Tom, and Chris felt every word was painful to him. "I was just thinking how you alone managed to survive the inferno on the promontory."

"I made a mess of things," said Bent unreflectingly. "I had the two farthest tanks, and one of the detonators didn't work. It wasn't easy to fix it in the dark, and it delayed me long enough to save my life. The others were all boarding the boat when the Germans opened fire!"

"How did you get away?" Tom said.

"I hid behind the tanks and took advantage of the confusion. They were all down by the boat; it was easy enough for me to get away by land. The others all lay around the big iron gate. They had managed to blow it up, but they got no farther. I don't think any of them were alive. That rotten detonator could easily have torn my head off, but it saved me instead. Paul must have been one of the ones killed there."

"Perhaps not. He may not even have been there!"

"What do you mean?"

"I mean that even though Paul made the plans, he didn't have to take part in the action. It's only a coincidence that you and I know each other. We know none of the others. Paul may be someone we have never seen. It is strange the guards could be taken so much by surprise that your group managed to blow up the oil tanks."

"And that the planes strafed the wrong targets," added Bent.

"That, in any case, is no mystery," Tom answered harshly. "It was part of the plan that two boats filled with gasoline-soaked sacks were to be set on fire shortly before the attack—the one a hundred meters south and the other a hundred meters north of the base. I know the boats were set on fire because I saw them. By the time the bombers arrived, they had been pulled ashore. That is why half the town is burning tonight. Can't you see the fiendishness behind it all? Not only was the base saved from a pounding, but the town was punished instead. Hundreds must be homeless or dead. This is a terror you can feel. Damn the Allies!"

Bent did not appear to be listening.

"Why weren't you out there?" he asked.

"I was there at the right time." Tom's eyes narrowed. "It was you, the boat group, the tank group, and the other group who got there at the wrong time."

"I knew nothing about the boats."

"I did—I wasn't the radio operator for that one group alone—and Paul knew, of course."

"I am glad," said Bent. "I am glad I do not know who Paul is."

"I am, too," said Tom.

Chris had been burning to ask a question, and he could keep it to himself no longer. "Why hasn't the Gestapo been here?"

"What did you say?" Tom almost jumped on him. "Has the Gestapo been at your house?"

Chris was on the verge of tears. How could he have forgotten to say that! It was hard for him to find the words. "They surrounded the house," he said falteringly.

Tom stamped his foot. "The devil take you schoolboys," he bellowed as he snatched up the machine gun.

Bent paled noticeably as he sat up quickly.

"It's my fault."

"I have no use for your explanations now," Tom said furiously. "Pray God that you won't need them later."

He tore a windbreaker down from the row of hooks in the hall. "Be ready to follow me when I come back." He turned off the light, and they heard him open the back door.

Chris almost hoped he would hear shots. Anything was better than the painful silence between him and his brother. Then Tom was in the room again.

"Can you manage?" he said roughly to Bent.

"I'll manage," Bent replied.

"Here!" Tom handed him his gun. He had picked it up outside.

"Now let's go." He locked the front door, turned out the lights, and herded them through the kitchen.

"Lucky it's snowing," he snapped as he locked the door behind them, "almost too lucky!"

Bent said nothing. The two of them walked side by side up the steep incline behind the house, Tom with his machine gun dangling across his chest and Bent with his right hand clenched hard inside his jacket.

Chris walked behind them. He felt quite alone.

3

CHRIS felt as if they had walked for hours when Tom finally stopped. They had struggled through tall thickets of juniper, jumped from boulder to boulder, waded through shoulder-deep snow—climbing steadily all the time. They more or less carried Bent between them the last stretch of the way.

They had reached a copse of pine trees when Tom said, "This is it!"

In spite of the darkness and the snow, Chris could see that there was nothing there.

Yet there was something. Once a colossal stone-slide must have come crashing down from the mountaintop. Now the huge boulders lay strewn about like rock candy.

This was a strange place to camp.

Tom laughed silently at Chris's confusion and said he was going to play Ali Baba.

"Open Sesame!" he said as he bent down and rolled a stone aside.

There wasn't much to see in the snowdrifts. After Tom

26

turned his flashlight toward the spot, Chris managed to make out a hole that led steeply down into the darkness.

"Our home for the time being," Tom said grandly. "I'll go down first."

It was necessary for him to do this, for though the cave was spacious, they would never have found the hidden room without him for a guide. There were sharp rocks jutting out of the walls; there were passages and pitfalls—it was altogether strange.

Finally they stood in a room that Tom lit by pulling a cord, and they could hardly believe their eyes. There were no jewels glistening on the walls, but later they discovered chests full of priceless treasures.

This room deep in the mountain had walls of a sort. They were made of sacks and straw matting. There was a wooden floor and a ceiling. A naked bulb dangling from a wire lit up the room. Even in his exhausted state, Chris was greatly impressed.

"And now for some heat!" Tom turned on an electric heater. Chris felt the warmth as he walked toward it.

"The electricity," Tom explained, gesturing around him, "comes from those batteries, and the batteries are charged by this dynamo. You have to spend a couple of hours every day turning the crank, but then there is heat and light for the rest of the day. Besides, it's good exercise. Quite an invention, don't you think?"

Bent was still so bewildered that he could only murmur it was marvelous, and marvelous was hardly the word! It was too good to be true. Chris was even more sure of this when Tom turned on the radio. Their own and most of the others' had been taken by the Nazis. There was a broadcast coming from London.

The announcer said, "Large contingents of Russian soldiers have crossed the Oder in the Küstrin area, and Marshall Zhukov has launched a massive attack on Berlin."

It was Friday, April 20, 1945.

Chris did not fully realize the meaning of those words, but Bent and Tom thumped each other on the back and Tom even cut a few capers. Then he dived into a box and brought out some cans and glasses. They drank a happy "skoal."

"We're going to win!" They held up two fingers making Churchill's V for victory sign. Chris had often chalked the sign secretly on billboards and on walls. He knew what it meant.

Tom opened a two-pound can of corned beef for each of them, and that was barely enough.

"Beef from the Pampas." Tom sighed blissfully. "Sent all the way from Argentina for this glorious meal!"

They ate it cold. Tom waved all questions aside—he would do the explaining later. Now all that mattered was satisfying their hunger. There was a lot of hunger to satisfy. For dessert they had cookies and chocolate. Chris felt sure he could have gone on eating until the next morning, but Tom stood up abruptly and pulled down a rucksack from a shelf.

"Sorry," he said. "It is getting close to one o'clock."

Bent asked, surprised, "What do you mean by that?"

"That London is waiting to hear from me." Tom walked toward the entrance.

28

"Why are you going out?" Bent's voice had a sharp edge again.

"Because the aerial doesn't work in here." Tom shook his head as if appalled at Bent's ignorance.

"Radio contact isn't too good in the first place. I have to be out in the open to get through. They will want to know all about this cursed mission."

"May I go with you?" Bent asked, and he stood up.

"Do you know the Morse code, or rather, the special signals that we use?"

Bent did not.

"Then you had better stay in and keep warm."

Tom turned on his heel and went out.

The two brothers eyed each other uncertainly. They could find nothing to talk about. They felt like strangers. Tom had come between them. So had the fire and the bombers that came too late.

Bent and Tom were watching each other. Tom was sending a message, but to whom—the Nazis or London?

Chris had no doubts as to what Bent thought, and the tension between the other two made him nervous. It was obvious which one of them would prove stronger if it came to a fight. Bent's injury was not serious, but he was not quite himself—not as Chris knew him. Tom was full of energy and confidence, but was he a traitor?

Chris could not believe that. Why had he fixed up the cave, then? It must have been hard work. There were four bunks with sleeping bags. Nothing grand, just rough timbers nailed together. Then there was the dynamo and the heater and the light. There was also a pile of English newspapers in pocket editions, printed on cigarette paper. Skis and plenty of clothing took up one corner. He had never seen such clothes before. They were white and as fine as silk. In one corner there was a pile of strange-looking boxes. The uppermost box was open, and Chris caught a glimpse of a machine gun in its greasy protective covering. Besides there was an abundant supply of food, Chris noticed to his satisfaction. Some of it was in packages that could be slipped directly into one's pockets, and some of it was in cans. There were bars of chocolate and meat and sausages.

That was all—except for a picture of His Majesty, the King of Norway. It was pinned onto an old coal sack.

Chris was not enthusiastic about the King, for his father had often spoken in favor of a republic. But the Nazis did not care much for the King either. Here again was something he did not understand.

Restlessly he picked up one of the English newspapers. It was the London *Times,* dated February 7. It contained an account of how the Japanese had been routed out of Manila and had lost forty-eight thousand men at Luzon. The Americans had lost seven thousand.

The names did not mean very much to Chris, but the numbers shocked him. This was not the way he had imagined war. In the newspapers he saw, not much was written about it. The local papers told of victories won by the Nazis, and lately they had mentioned retreats, but never defeats. Well, yes, defeats suffered by the Allies. But of course that was just propaganda.

Chris had never imagined for a moment that the Allies might lose the war, even though he wasn't exactly sure who

the Allies were and where they were fighting. He was familiar with death. He had seen his father lying on the carpet, had been beaten on the street by a soldier, and had been questioned endlessly. But these things concerned him alone. In the cave he suddenly realized that this war concerned the entire world.

Forty-eight thousand dead Japanese, seven thousand dead Americans—all in one area. How many were dying elsewhere?

Bent had fallen asleep on one of the bunks. The blood-soaked turban was coming loose.

After a while Tom returned, looking very grim.

"They knew all about it already," he said as he put down the rucksack.

Chris said nothing. What could he say! He turned his head toward Bent.

"Yes," said Tom, "we had better get some sleep. Maybe we will get orders tomorrow," he added.

Several days passed before the order to move on came. Each night Tom went out with the rucksack, and each time he returned, disappointed. "They must have other things than us on their minds."

Most of the time they sat glued to the radio, and Chris began to understand the catastrophe in which he now was so deeply involved. The showdown was clearly soon to come. In the West, the Allied armies were lined up along the Elbe and the Nordic seaports. In the East, the Russians hammered at the German defenses outside Berlin. The Americans were forcing the Japanese to a retreat in the Pacific. In occupied areas more patriots and hostages were being executed. All over the world people were being killed—great numbers of innocent people. After the sabotage action on the promontory, prominent citizens of the town had been shot. Chris felt hate swell up in him as he heard the speaker read the names of the dead, even though he knew none of the people.

Time dragged. The old newspapers were soon read, and only two hours at the crank kept the dynamo going. They were eager for their turns.

Bent recovered completely, and his relationship with Tom improved. It was only when Tom went out to send radio messages that Bent's suspicion was aroused again. And there was no mistaking Tom's despondency each time he had made contact. Chris dreaded the times Tom took the rucksack and left.

They found out all about the cave while they waited for orders. Centuries ago, gigantic stone slides had formed hidden pockets, rock shelves, ravines, and passages here. Tom had discovered them as a child, and he had had his cave in the mountain then, the way Chris had his house in the tree. Then make-believe became reality, and the cave became a safe hiding place for fugitives. In the beginning, most of them tried to escape to England. They got away by sailing across the North Sea in fishing boats, motorboats, or even rowboats. Now people were fleeing into the mountains. The Occupation army had had plans to recruit all young men the way they had done in other countries but had thought better of it. Very few, however, escaped the German work battalions. Strongholds, shelters, and machine-gun nests had to be built. Barbed-wire fencing had to be put up. Norway was

32

to be Hitler's final barricade, and the Norwegians were to be made to build it themselves. That was the way to humiliate a people.

"How can they do it!" Chris burst out one day when they were talking about it.

"You have no idea what they can do," Tom said shortly.

Bent looked very grave. "What we are experiencing now," he said, "has never happened before: boys are waging war on boys. I was only fifteen when I started delivering my father's illegal newspapers. I crept along stairways, praying no one would see me. I do not blame my father, for I know now that he was a lonely man. It seems to me I have never been young. I have always lived with fear: each time I boarded a streetcar, each time I walked through a door, each time I lay down to sleep. I knew I was doing something dangerous, but I did not know why it had to be that way. I did not know why until a very long time after they murdered him. I wonder if Father actually hated them? I believe he was a good person who revolted against injustice and brutality. I am afraid the hatred I feel is beginning to affect my mind. A terrible uncertainty keeps nagging me: was it I—because of some boyish clumsiness—who gave my father away?"

Tom sat silent for a long time. Finally he said, "You can be sure your father's death was no fault of yours. He was betrayed by the woman to whom he naïvely had entrusted the printing of his illegal newspaper."

"Does she have a scar over one eye?" Chris asked suddenly.

"Over the left eye, yes."

33

Tom continued. "We know her name, her address, and what she is up to."

"But she's still free," Bent interrupted.

"She goes free until she can be tried and convicted. She will not be able to do more harm."

"Hasn't she done enough?" Bent pounded the table furiously. Quietly Tom said, "This war is not a private feud for you and your family. Your father fought his own war. Maybe he was lonely, but he was not alone. Ten other illegal newspapers circulated at the same time in our little town. Even this hideout was ready then."

And Tom told them how it had happened. The weapons and supplies were brought into the bay by torpedo boats. Fishing boats transported the cargo to the shore, and then it was carried up to the cave at night. Now all supplies came by air. Large containers were dropped by parachute onto the mountain plateaus and distributed from there. The cave was just one of many stops along the way.

Couriers and others carrying out special missions still sailed across the North Sea. It was a perilous voyage, and some never got through. Young Norwegians escaped to the mountains. There were regular military units there under Allied command. They were effective forces awaiting the signal to strike.

For the three in the cave, the signal came through on the fourth night.

For once Tom was excited. "We're going over the mountain tomorrow night," he shouted. "They will be expecting us over on the other side on Wednesday morning."

Bent's eyes shone, and they shook hands.

34

4

NONE of them slept much. They went over the incidents of that disastrous night when the oil tanks on the promontory were set afire again and again—the night everything went wrong.

Obviously they had been betrayed. The Germans had been expecting them.

According to the plan, the sole mission of the attacking party was to distract the Nazis guarding the land side of the promontory, where the oil tanks were, long enough to allow the saboteurs to go ashore and reach the tanks they were to blow up.

Meanwhile, a third party was to set fire to the rowboats in the harbor to mark the target for the bombers. The bombers were to attack at the same moment the fake attack on the Nazi guards began.

The bombers had come too late, and the flaming rowboats had been moved from their designated positions. The party that had set fire to them had disappeared.

The most peculiar thing was that, with everything else going wrong, the Nazi guards were not prepared. Why hadn't they been tipped off? The attacking party had been able to delay the guards long enough for the saboteurs to blow up the oil tanks. They had gone ahead with this, even though the bombers had not arrived.

The more they talked, the more questions they had. Why had the Gestapo surrounded the house on the hillside? Why were there only German soldiers on the promontory? Why wasn't the Gestapo there, too? Could there possibly have been two separate actions, independent of each other? Could that explain why Tom had been left out? That did not sound likely. There had to be a traitor, and the traitor could be no one but Paul, this Paul none of them knew. Why had he spared Tom?

"Possibly because he was a friend," said Tom thoughtfully, "but *who?*"

The day was as restless as the night had been sleepless. They had no more preparations to make. The equipment had been ready since their first day in the cave. The skis had long since been carried to the mouth of the cave. All they had to do was wait.

Bent had cast sidelong glances at the box with the machine guns, but Tom had cut him off, remarking that the weapons were at the disposal of the military organization in town. Bent would have to make do with his pistol.

Chris had never crossed the mountain before. It was an enormous mountain, craggy and broken. Once on top, the mountain plateaus were good for skiing, but the skis had to be carried up there and back down. Chris had always thought of it as a useless mountain, but now it was to prove itself useful.

The three in the cave were to be moved safely now, like chessmen, into the next square. In spite of his excitement, Tom did not disclose what the next move would be. Maybe he did not know. They started out shortly before midnight.

Tom's cave had two exits, like a rabbit's burrow, and one was worse than the other.

"The good thing about the cave is that you can always get away," boasted Tom. "If the Nazis should by chance blunder down into one of the exits, there's time enough to escape through the other—they are a hundred meters apart —even time enough to get a good head start into the woods. I may be too cautious, not allowing cooking in the cave, but why take any chances! Steam can tell tales. It can melt the snow or rise like a smoke signal. Now only warm air leaves the cave, and it cools off by the time it reaches the far exit."

They came out of the cave high above the pine woods. Tom carefully covered up the opening. It was not snowing, but there were rings around the moon. There would be a heavy snowfall during the night. They were dressed in the white coveralls and English boots of fine leather that Chris had seen in the cave earlier. Each of them carried three-day rations. Chris had stuffed the small packages into his pockets skeptically.

The climb was exhausting but without incident. They rested for the first time at the timberline. Bent and Tom lit cigarettes. Chris brought out a bar of chocolate from the little supply he had stashed away.

The town below them lay ghostly and still. Only the moon shone coldly on thousands of lifeless windowpanes. Now and then searchlights swept the harbor. Afterward the darkness seemed blacker.

The moon was still out when they reached the mountain plateau and could put on their skis, but a wind with snow on its breath began to blow.

The plateau stretched as far as they could see, fairylike and beautiful in the white light, but treacherous. Shadows distorted the contours. As always, Tom led the way. The hard-packed snow was icy and sharp as glass. The slightest fall could prove fatal. They had no time to lose. They were to reach the meeting place at dawn—no earlier and no later.

The snow overtook them on the plateau, and it came in a blizzard. Howling viciously, it threw itself upon them and forced them to seek shelter under a ledge. Even with the flashlight, they could barely see a meter ahead. Chris was bitterly cold, but he was careful not to say anything. He was tired of being told that he was just a boy. Tom and Bent swore loud and long. After about an hour, the moon was once more visible in the ragged sky. The slick, icy mountain plateau was covered with enormous drifts of powdery snow that made the going rougher than before and more dangerous.

It grew light before they began the descent. By now they should have been at their destination.

"We're allowed to turn back, but I will not. Besides, we can't find the cave after this confounded snowstorm."

"Then what are we waiting for?" Bent sent Tom a quick look.

It was a long way down. Through the frosty mist Chris could barely make out the railway town they were supposed to reach. Long before they got down, the sun would disperse the morning mist. Now a snowstorm would have come in handy. On the other side of the valley, the mountains soared up into the sky. The blood pounded at Chris's temples, and he breathed with difficulty. He wanted to sink back into the snow and sleep.

A shove in the back interrupted his despondent thoughts. Tom had already taken off, and Bent followed with a hoarse shout at Chris. Chris mustered all the strength and courage he had left and started a giddy dive into the deep valley.

He made it, but later—he didn't know how much later—when he rammed into the others at the edge of the wood, his legs could carry him no more. He fell into the snow and cried with fatigue. They were fairly safe in the woods, but they had no time to rest. They buried the skis that were only a burden now. Half carrying Chris between them, Tom and Bent ran frantically. They did not stop until they reached the bottom of the valley. Tom gripped the machine gun firmly, pushed the branches of the pine trees aside, and looked out cautiously. Then he stepped out onto the mountain road.

A soldier appeared on the opposite side of the road. He was pointing a machine gun at Tom.

"*Hände hoch!*" he said.

5

No shots were fired, but Bent had his gun ready.

"Cicero," said Tom.

"Caesar," answered the stranger.

"Why the comedy," said Tom angrily. "You knew darn well we were coming."

"All hell has broken loose. They've gone nuts over that sabotage action in town. All the roads are blocked."

"Lucky it was you who blocked this one."

Chris clambered sheepishly out of the ditch he had thrown himself into.

The stranger continued, "You're late. I was worried. By now you should have been on the fjord boat. They had to sail without you. What happened?"

"Nothing! I had counted on the moonlight, but we ran into a snowstorm instead. What do we do now?"

"We must get away from here, fast. The only possible means of transportation is a German military train."

"Just what we need!" said Tom with a hollow laugh.

"I have thought it over and decided that the train is safe enough. They won't search their own train."

"I hope you're right."

"Let's get started then."

The stranger walked into the woods. He led them in a wide detour around the railroad station and through the valley. Once they had left the settled area behind, they crossed the railroad tracks. The woods were dense on both sides, and the mountain rose steeply above them. Chris shuddered at the thought of having to climb up that way. He was not so tired any more, but he was beginning to be hungry.

They followed the tracks to the beginning of a sharp curve. Their guide looked at his watch and said, "The train should be here in fifteen minutes. It will slow down for the curve. Boarding it should be easy. You are to jump on the caboose before it takes the curve. The view from the first car will then be obstructed. The train is carrying supplies and troops for the defense of Berlin. It will be derailed up in the mountains. We don't think there will be any survivors. The drop is more than a hundred meters to the valley. There are six hundred soldiers on board and plenty of military policemen to guard them—presumably to prevent their deserting. The MP's may enter the last car from time to time, to have a quick drink, but there is no reason to believe that they will look into the cubbyhole at the very back where you are to hide. But if they should, you know what to do."

He rapped the barrel of the machine gun meaningfully. Then he continued. "The train crew is made up of the engineer, the fireman, and the brakeman. The brakeman doesn't

41

know you are coming, and it will be your business to convince him that you are all right. The derailment will take place on a stretch of track up a sharp incline. The train will move no faster than you can walk. Getting off will be easier than getting on. The Norwegian crew and some Norwegian soldiers will join you. I have no way of letting them know about you, but the code words for the action are 'Stalingrad' and 'Coventry.' Is that clear?"

Bent and Tom nodded gravely. Both held on to their weapons firmly. The hostility between them was gone. Chris was more curious. Why didn't anybody ask about the man's uniform? It was brown. On the right sleeve was the Norwegian flag, and on the beret were the initials of the King. Chris had never seen a uniform like it before, and he said so.

"I belong to the Allied Forces," said the stranger stiffly. "If I were in civilian clothes and got caught, I would be considered a partisan—and treated accordingly."

Chris had more questions to ask, but they heard the train coming. The heavy bumping of the wheels as they rolled over the joints rumbled through the rails.

The man in the brown uniform smiled for the first time. "Good luck!" he said and saluted. Then he walked into the woods and disappeared.

Tom took charge once more. He intended to board the train from the left side, open the door, and hold up the brakeman. Bent and Chris were to get on from the other side and stand on the steps until he gave the all-clear signal.

They managed to hide between the trees as the train came into sight. The engine wheezed tiredly. Chris tingled with

42

excitement, and the rest of his tiredness vanished. He fidg-eted impatiently while the heavy cars crawled slowly by—first a never-ending line of freight cars with field guns and antiaircraft guns, then finally the passenger cars. The blinds were drawn, but Chris could easily imagine the green-uniformed soldiers he hated so bitterly inside. They were probably guzzling beer out of bottles and stuffing them-selves with their disgusting sausages. They thought they were going home to defend Berlin. He knew they were going to die.

The engine would be derailed first. It would plunge into the valley, taking all the cars with it to destruction. The men in the green uniforms had nothing to hope for. Maybe the Allied planes were bombing Berlin at this very moment. They would have nothing to go home to anyway.

The caboose rolled into the curve. With a leap they were beside it. Bent swung himself up on the steps first. Then Chris jumped on and held tight.

With his other hand, Chris grabbed an iron ring and pulled himself up beside Bent. Through the frosty window they could see Tom standing with his machine gun pressed against the brakeman's belly. Chris looked away. He felt chilled, and the iron ring he was holding gave him the un-pleasant feeling of being caught. He had forgotten to put on his mittens, and his hand was sticking to the metal.

Tom gave the signal from inside. They could enter. Bent opened the door and went in first. He had his gun in his hand. Chris's hand was frozen to the iron ring, and blood oozed from it when he pulled it loose. Bent reached out and hauled him in.

Chris could have wept—not so much over the pain as over his own stupidity. He did not dare look his brother in the eye, much less Tom. He stood in the middle of the narrow compartment with the blood dripping down his white coveralls and wished he were somewhere else.

"I'm sorry," he said hesitantly.

"Idiot!" exclaimed his brother.

Tom said nothing, but there was a trace of scorn on his face. Chris realized he would never like Tom.

The brakeman came to his rescue. "I have a first-aid kit," he stammered. He was still trembling from the shock Tom had given him. He opened a cabinet on the wall and brought out boric-acid solution, some cotton, and a bandage.

The brakeman was a timid little man. He was anxious to help and happy to have something to do. He put a neat bandage on Chris's bleeding hand and gently pushed him down on a folding chair. "Just rest for a while, my boy, and you'll soon feel fine."

Tom had watched with increasing displeasure. He asked now, "Is the door locked?"

"Which door?"

"The door to the passenger car, of course."

"Why should it be locked? I didn't know you were coming."

"Lock it then!"

"Won't that look suspicious? I'll have to open it in any case—if they turn up."

"Maybe you're right."

It was the first time Chris had heard Tom admit that somebody else could be right.

"When is it going to be?" Tom asked.

"In four hours, maybe five." The brakeman shrugged his shoulders. "It all depends."

"What do you mean by that?"

"We have to have an extra engine coupled on before we start up into the mountains, and that takes time."

He gestured over his shoulder at the rear window. "It'll push."

"I haven't heard anything about two engines." Tom sounded doubtful.

"Neither had we until this morning. The Germans suddenly demanded that ten extra cars with antiaircraft guns be coupled on. That's why we're dragging along like this. And they're the same guns that were hauled the other way week before last. They hadn't even been unloaded! Strange people!"

"Really." Tom did not seem to find it interesting to discuss the conduct of the Germans any further. He dropped the subject.

"We haven't had anything to eat for a long time," he said in a surprisingly friendly fashion as he reached for the rucksack.

"Oh, no you don't!" The brakeman stopped him with an authority that almost seemed absurd, considering his humble appearance. "As long as you are in my car, you must be my guests. The trip over the mountains can take three days and three nights in these disturbed times, so I have plenty of food for all of us. Sit down and let Papa take care of everything."

Before Tom could protest, he found himself sitting on the

other folding chair in the tiny compartment. Chris could see that it was difficult for Bent to keep from smiling. He himself found it safest to watch the brakeman up front as he juggled professionally with cups and lunch boxes and Thermos jugs filled with hot coffee. Soon they were sitting around an empty oil drum, luxuriously covered with packages of butter, cheese, white bread, and steaming cups of coffee. They ate while the brakeman rambled on about how lucky he had been on his last trip. Fate had planned things so considerately. Besides the antiaircraft guns, they had also freighted a carload of Bulgarian leaf tobacco. It tasted horrible, but on the black market it was worth its weight in gold —if not more!

"Did you steal . . ." Chris stopped nervously before he had finished the sentence, but the brakeman only laughed.

"My friend, you don't steal from the Germans—you take what is your due!"

"Without being caught?" Chris asked in surprise.

"My boy"—the brakeman winked at him—"the tobacco had been under way for a long time, and it was tied in bales with rusty iron wire, so there had to be some shrinkage. Even Nazis understand that! I remember . . ."

Tom interrupted him. "When were you told that the train was to be sabotaged?"

"This morning. I was stopped on my way to the station by two men in railwaymen's uniforms. They escorted me all the way to the station. There was so much confusion with all the soldiers that no one noticed them."

"And you spoke with no one else?"

"Just the boys on the crew. We all had agreed, of course."

"And you did?"

"Naturally."

"But what if you hadn't?" Chris asked curiously.

"They knew we would not refuse." The brakeman was proud. "They knew all about us. And to think that the Germans first ordered us to make the trip yesterday afternoon. Things were well planned. I am only sorry I didn't get a message through to the missus. She's all right. Now she will have to act well bred and spend money on mourning clothes, not go to the movies, and be ready to burst into tears every time anyone says how sorry they are. We are not cut out for the part. My missus and I, we are not well bred. We are lower class."

The brakeman turned his thumb down. Chris liked to listen to him. He had opened the door to another world. Chris's life in the house on the hillside had been irregular these last years, but basically it had not changed much. Chris could not remember his mother. She had left them when he was a little boy, and her name was never mentioned in the house. Their father had looked after them lovingly. They had lacked nothing. Even after their father's death, they had led a privileged life.

There were many things Chris wanted to ask the brakeman about, but they would have to wait. He felt warm and good after the meal, and the tiredness after the exertions of the night before was getting the better of him. Sitting on the folding chair, he began to nod. The brakeman's voice faded farther and farther away through the monotonous click-clack of the wheels.

"I could of course send her a card from the station when we stop, but I'm not much for writing. Besides, she's a blabbermouth! A nice bit to gossip about: I haven't been

47

bumped off, but I lead a secret life! For us life has always been hard, and the Germans haven't made it easier. We have to take things as they come; that's what I've been taught. I ask myself whether it would have been different if the British —they had planned to, you know—had come first. For us at the short end of the stick, I mean. We can't afford to think about who is right."

Chris slept.

He was awakened by someone pushing his head against the dirty window. He wanted to scream but could not. Bent's hands were over his mouth. Tom stood pressed against the wall on the other side, with his machine gun pointed at the half-open door. His eyes glowed strangely, his lips were pressed hard together, and his face had tightened to an unnatural whiteness.

6

THE brakeman wasn't there, but Chris could hear voices up front. They spoke German, and he recognized words like *zigaretten, Schnaps, englische Schweinhunde,* and *verdammte Sabotören.*

Chris felt clammy, and he began to tremble. He had an uncontrollable urge to move around, to stamp his feet, or to hit somebody. His fear turned into a pain that shot through his limbs. Finally to his great relief he heard the words, *"Auf Wiedersehen,"* and a door was slammed shut.

"That was close!" Bent slackened his grip and wiped the sweat off his brow. "What did he want?"

"He was just bored." The brakeman stood in the doorway with a wide smile on his face. "And he wanted to know how much longer the trip would take."

It struck Chris that the brakeman's mildness had given way to something shrewd. He would probably turn out to be much smarter than he chose to look. He did not try to hide that he was proud of having warded off the danger.

"He even poured me a drink of *Schnaps,*" the brakeman

49

boasted, "and he lit my cigarette! The best way to start a conversation with a German is to ask for a cigarette. He walked straight into the trap. However, one must stop them in time, or before you know it, they will have you looking at pictures of their wives and children. Not for me! The British now, what do you think of them? I'm not good at German, but one catches on to a word here and there on these long trips.

"These damned green devils are not the only ones who think that the British are pigs. You should have heard what people had to say after the attack on the submarine base. The town is still in an uproar—they are practically on the side of the Germans!"

"When do we stop for that extra engine?" Tom interrupted the brakeman's flow of talk as if he hadn't listened to any of it.

"In twenty minutes." The brakeman looked out. "It can't be much more. We have plenty of time." He busied himself, tidying up after their meal, and then he waved them into a small cubicle. "It won't be too comfortable," he said apologetically, "but it will be safe!"

Much could be said to the credit of the brakeman, but he was no stickler for order, and his lack of order stood them in good stead at this point. Tarpaulins lay in heaps on the floor among rubber boots, oilcans, tools, coils of rope, and electric cables. Overalls hung on rusty nails, and a cupboard yawned with its door wide open.

"I think the cupboard will be right for the boy," said the master of this mess. "You two hulks can crawl under the tarpaulins."

50

Tom scowled, and the brakeman hurriedly added that absolutely nobody would be entering the caboose. When the train stopped, everyone would stay put, but there was no way of keeping some busybody on the platform from peeking in. He was going to talk to the crew on the extra engine.

Chris could see that the last remark definitely did not suit Tom, but none of them raised any objections, and soon all three were well hidden.

The brakeman left them with a final warning. "Coupling an extra engine on normally takes just a few minutes, but don't worry, even if it should take a half an hour." Under no circumstances were they to come out of hiding before he said so. Then he left, shutting the door carefully behind him.

The train had slowed down. It wheezed and grunted before stopping with a heavy sigh. Sharp orders were given outside. There was a running and stamping of heavy boots on the frozen snow and a snorting and hissing from the extra engine that was moving in from behind. The caboose groaned as the iron buffers clanged together loudly.

Chris tried to peek through the keyhole, but he only caught a glimpse of the sky. It had begun to snow, and he wondered whether that would be an advantage once they got higher up into the mountains.

The guard blew his whistle, and the long row of cars jerked back and forth on the rails. The engine let off steam in short, shrill blasts.

At last they were on their way. Everything was going according to plan—or was it? Didn't the brakeman hesitate before he called them out. There was no mistaking the look in his eyes—he was afraid!

51

"What has happened?" Chris exclaimed, even before Bent and Tom had crawled out of their dirty hiding places. "Have you seen a ghost?"

"Almost!" The brakeman faltered. It was nearly impossible to hear his voice above the noise of the extra engine.

"Answer properly, man!" Tom had jumped up and grabbed the brakeman by the shoulder. "What's the matter!"

"I do not know them."

"Do not know who?"

"The fireman and the engineer."

"Does that mean anything?"

"It means that they are strangers!"

"Did you speak with them?"

"No! I may be stupid," said the brakeman as he drew himself up straight, "but not that stupid!"

"Then you don't know if they speak Norwegian."

"They speak Norwegian, if that's any guarantee."

"Not much!" Tom spoke in a quiet voice, but there was a threatening look in his eyes. The brakeman had calmed down by now, so he pulled away from Tom's grip and lit one of his stinking German cigarettes in a manner that clearly showed he was in no mood to be insulted.

Bent tried to reason with them. "We have to trust one another," he said, "regardless of whether we can trust others."

"Right!" the brakeman agreed somewhat maliciously. "There's nothing you can do about it." He paused as if a bright idea had just occurred to him and then continued.

52

"But I can, so just take it easy. I'm not saying that I will, but while we are waiting, maybe you gents with good breeding and an education can answer this question."

"Make it fast and short, then!" Tom was still aggressive.

"Take your time," the brakeman said with quiet composure. "There's no hurry, and the problem is very important to me. When I get to thinking that all these young men soon will have to die—not that they haven't done enough harm; get that straight—I get to thinking that with one single move I could save their lives. But if I shut my eyes and let things happen, am I the one who is responsible or is God responsible? Or is the King, or a man whose name I don't know?"

Tom looked at him blankly. "Don't think too much," he said. "The wise will think for us."

"Will we die?"

"Possibly."

"What for?"

"We didn't start this war"—Tom leaned wearily against the rumbling wall—"and none of us wants to kill the men in the cars up ahead. But do we want to be killed instead? No, we want to survive." He struck his hand against a sooty windowpane. "Maybe there's a woman in Potsdam or Dresden waiting for her husband to come home. But there are also women waiting in Okinawa, in Newcastle, and in Bergen. That's what it's all about. We can't afford to be generous or to give way to our feelings."

"Isn't that a convenient way to look at it?"

"We can discuss that later." Tom brushed the brakeman

53

off. "Right now we have other things to attend to. Is there no chance that you could be wrong about the two new men?"

"No chance at all; I have worked on this line for twenty years."

"They could have come from another line, from one of the private railroad lines."

"Yes, I suppose."

"That's what we will think then: there wasn't time enough to find the right crew among the railroad men, so the leader of this sabotage action must have decided to put on his own men. That sounds likely. Is there any way of getting in touch with them?"

"No."

"Good! Now to our part of the job!"

"My part of the job?" drawled the brakeman. "I have none. I just have to keep my eyes open. Two hundred meters before we get to the spot where the train is to be dynamited, a pair of crossed skis will be stuck in the left bank. That's the signal for me to jump off into the snow and lie low until the whole show is over. I think that you three should join me."

He smiled. The genial atmosphere was restored. Chris contributed his last bars of chocolate, and the brakeman coaxed them to eat the rest of his food. He said it might be some time before they ate again.

Chris was not afraid. On the contrary, he felt a growing excitement. They did not talk. There was too much noise in the small cubicle at the very back of the caboose for conversation. They all sat thinking their private thoughts. It was

54

still snowing, but even when it stopped occasionally, there wasn't much to see. The train snaked through tunnels, and only glimpses of the massive white mountains and the deep valley below could be seen.

When there were just a few minutes left to go, the brakeman repeated the instructions.

"Jump well away, with your weight forward. Remember, your weight forward." He would jump first, then Chris and Bent, and finally Tom.

They passed the marker. The brakeman stood with the door slightly ajar. He shouted a cheery, "See you soon," and vanished into the snowy fog. A moment later, Chris landed in the snow. For one split second he heard the roar of the engine; then it was gone. He struggled like a madman to get clear of the snow. He wanted to see it happen regardless of the orders to lie low.

Fifty meters ahead, the train lumbered straight toward its destruction.

The explosion was not so violent as he had imagined it would be—not the first one. The muffled sound was rather a disappointment. To Chris it looked as if the engine rose into the air like a rearing horse. Before it toppled over onto its side, there was a new terrible, ear-splitting explosion. The earth trembled, and the sky was full of huge rocks that sailed slowly down to the bottom of the valley.

"My God!" said the dazed brakeman beside him. "They have blown away the entire mountainside!"

Through the choking smoke that billowed around them, they caught glimpses of the gaping hole in the mountain. The rails curled back like ragged paper streamers in the quivering air. The echo rolled through the mountains. The engine was gone, and so were many of the freight cars, but others stood still and intact on the rails, including all the passenger cars. No, they were not standing still; good God in heaven, they were moving! The extra engine pushed them unrelentingly toward the chasm.

"Almighty God," the brakeman said with a terrified gasp, "forgive us our sins."

Unable to move, Chris watched the chugging engine. This was madness—unbelievable, horrible, and ghastly. With each grind of its heavy pistons the empty engine—for it must have been empty—drove the men in green uniforms closer to death.

No one could stop it now.

There was an unnerving silence within the train. The explosions had shaken up the old wooden passenger cars, but the soldiers were behind drawn curtains and didn't know the cause. At that point they must have been diving for shelter automatically.

The saboteurs fired at the train. An explosion, set off by bullets striking the Germans' grenades, shattered the first car. Too late, the soldiers rushed at the doors and windows. They tried to shoot their way out, to squeeze their way out; they used their rifle butts and one another as pile drivers. It was no use. They ran straight into a rain of bullets. None of them got out alive.

Screaming and cursing wildly, they rolled over the precipice, carload after carload, until only the engine was left. It tipped over and hurtled after them with a tearing sound, and halfway down it hit a ledge and exploded. New explosions sounded from the valley. Huge tongues of flame licked upward. But the snow was deep and quiet. Soon the smoke reached the stunned men watching.

There were eight of them, and they stood huddled close together. The men from the extra engine had joined them. Beneath their railroad overalls, they wore brown uniforms like the soldier who had accompanied them to the train.

"That explains it," thought Chris dully to himself, and began walking toward the edge of the crater with the others.

No one talked. The brakeman cried.

7

SUDDENLY there was a crowd of men up ahead. They seemed to pop out of nowhere, all of them in white coveralls, carrying machine guns. They seemed to be looking for signs of life below, but there were none. A few of these men came toward Chris and his group. The men from the extra engine walked forward. They all saluted, then stood around and talked. Occasionally they tossed their heads in the direction of Chris, Bent, and Tom. Chris wanted to go up to them, but his brother held him back. One of the men from the mountain was the spokesman, obviously the leader. He had an automatic weapon that was bigger than the weapons the others carried.

"At last I get to see a Bren gun," Bent whispered excitedly. "With a gun like that, you can shoot down a Messerschmitt." Then he added, "With a little luck!"

It was a fearful weapon, more than a meter long—a stark, deadly weapon.

Chris wished he had a Bren gun.

58

The men hailed them.

"Hello there, what are you waiting for?"

What were they waiting for? Chris prickled with excitement, but Bent and Tom hesitated. Was there an uncertain look about Tom? Nonsense, Tom was never unsure of himself!

The leader was older than Bent but younger than Tom. He did not look pleased, but worried and tired. His voice was harsh.

"Well done," he said approvingly to the railwaymen. None of them replied. They stood like lost schoolboys, scraping their feet in the snow, though each one of them could have been the father of the soldier, who now turned to address Tom.

"Who the hell are you!" he said angrily.

Tom straightened up.

"Coventry," he said, and slammed his heels together so hard that Chris had to laugh. Even the soldier with the Bren gun almost smiled.

"You can stop playing cops and robbers," he said a little less harshly. "What I want to know is who sent you, where you got your weapons and equipment, and what made you think we are running a kindergarten here in the mountains."

Chris was not easy to offend that day. He smiled cheerfully, quite convinced that from now on nothing could go wrong.

Tom was not happy about the situation. He was shaken, and he stammered as he accounted for their actions. The stammer irritated him, so that his explanations became too long and involved. When he finally got to the part about the fjord boat they missed, he was sharply interrupted by the leader.

"I know the rest. You were to come by a different route. I only expected the railway crew to be on the train. But we'll manage. We do not have enough skis, but the snow is hard, and a couple of my boys will be the better for a nice long walk."

The final remark was uttered with a smile, but then he looked severe again.

"Welcome to the Free Norwegian Forces," he said shortly. "It's a long way to the camp. It must be understood that each man does his best. Our mission has been of utmost importance and has been carried out successfully, but we will tolerate no departure from the established program."

Chris looked uncertainly at Bent and Tom, but they both seemed impressed by the situation, Bent most of all. Tom stared stiffly ahead, and Chris thought it would probably be some time before Tom smiled again.

Another man stepped up beside the leader and said, "You can turn in your weapons and follow me." Neither Bent nor Tom protested. They walked after him.

There was not much to see at the gaping crater except smoke-blacked snow. Huge rocks lay strewn about, jumbled together with bits of railroad ties and pieces of wrecked freight cars. Soon, only the curled tracks and the yawning hole in the mountainside would bear witness to the catastrophe. Chris ventured out to the edge of the crater but was called back to try on some skis before he managed to see anything.

60

There were about twenty men in the group, all young. A couple of them asked for news from the town but soon realized that they themselves were better informed.

Within five minutes they all had put on their skis, all except the soldiers who needed a walk, and the two men from the extra engine. Chris guessed they were in their middle thirties. They looked strong and athletic. He wondered why their faces were so lined and furrowed.

The big Bren gun and some other heavy-caliber guns were placed beside Tom's rucksack on a runner sled. Then they started off in single file. Though Chris was in the middle of the line, he could see neither the first nor the last man through the whirling snow. Behind him he could see two men pulling the sled with the weapons. At the very back, the men without skis walked on the hard-packed trail that the skis had made. The climb was steep in the beginning. Chris was between the brakeman and Bent, and it amused him to listen to the brakeman cursing his skis.

"I was a regular clown on skis, even as a boy," he said gruffly, "and that was a long time ago. Since then I have forgotten more than I ever learned. Good thing, too, because it seems we are to start a fresh new life, eh, boy?"

"As soldiers," Chris answered happily.

"Don't you say things like that," the brakeman said soberly. "Let the grownups fight the war, and enjoy your youth while you're still young. You will never be young again. Remember that. You can be young and have a bad time of it, but you can take it because you are young. Later it gets tougher."

Chris said, "What was it like when you were young?"

61

"Rough, just that, rough! There was a war on then, too. My father was a seaman. The damned Germans blew up his ship. I haven't forgotten. No, my boy, I haven't forgotten."

Chris shuddered. The sudden hatred in the middle-aged railwayman's voice was as unexpected as it was uncompromising. Did everyone hate? Did the Germans hate, too? No, he didn't think so. They did not burn and kill out of hatred but rather out of sheer viciousness—it had to be viciousness.

After the first steep climb, the going was easier. It was still snowing so heavily that Chris had a hard time getting his bearings. He felt he should be able to tell what direction they were taking, but all he knew was that they were way above the timberline.

The leader dropped back to inquire how things were going. He was mainly interested in the railwaymen, but they seemed to manage surprisingly well.

"Great," answered the brakeman when he was told that there were several hours to go yet. "I'll be champion before we get there."

A young man with a tired face nodded. "You will have to be!"

Chris liked the leader, although he wished he hadn't taken their weapons away from them. Didn't the man believe Tom's story or didn't he trust Tom? It was not a pleasant thought, but Tom had acted strangely down on the tracks. Chris turned to Bent.

"Do you think he suspects?"

"Suspects what?" His brother looked at him in surprise.

"Suspects Tom. He acted so peculiarly before."

"Oh, stop it. Anyone can get nervous. I was nervous myself!"

"But then why did they take away our weapons?"

"How should I know why?" His brother sounded irritated. "You think too much!"

Chris knew that Bent, too, had been thinking along these lines. He would hardly have been so edgy otherwise. Bent was not about to discuss the matter with Chris—that was all. He was only a boy! Chris rammed his ski poles so hard into the snow that he ran into the brakeman ahead of him. The brakeman laughed good-naturedly.

"Hey there, take it easy. I'm not a champion yet, you know. The wife should see me now. She would never believe I was such a bag of muscles."

They got a warning toward evening. It had stopped snowing. The cloud banks hung low and sluggishly over the mountains. They threaded their way through a gorge between two mountain ranges. The line of skiers twisted on along the gentle rise like a snake.

"A dangerous snake," Chris thought with satisfaction, "a viper!"

Suddenly an order was yelled from up front. "Take cover, planes!"

The order spread through the ranks, and the soldiers dived into the snow. It was as if an enormous scythe had mowed them down. The roar of plane engines sounded above. In a flash a German fighter plane came into view below the cloud bank at the far end of the valley. It continued across the valley and disappeared. Soon the noise died away.

"They are looking for us," said Bent as they stood brushing the snow off themselves.

"Why didn't we fire?" stammered Chris.

63

"Are you crazy?" Bent was truly dismayed. "It would be like asking to be slaughtered. We want to live through the war, don't we?"

Chris did not answer. His teeth chattered, and he began to shake all over. He realized he had been afraid, and the thought made him furious.

His brother thumped him comfortingly on the back. "You have to get scared sometime or other; anything else would be unnatural."

"Because I'm only a boy," snapped Chris.

Bent smiled sadly. "You are a boy no longer," he said.

Shortly afterward they stopped to rest at a mountain cottage. It was practically snowed under, and Chris did not realize it was there until he was almost upon it. Some of the men must have gone on ahead, for there was a great pot of steaming soup on an old stove. Each man was given a tin mug and a package of rations like the one Chris had been given in the cave. Now he would find out what was in them. He had been curious to know for a long time. They sat on their skis outside the hut and ate.

In the package there were crackers, corned beef, chocolate, a tea bag, a bag of lemon drops, a pack of cigarettes, and a roll of sugar. The men complained loudly about the meat, but Chris thought it was a treat and ate two portions before he was satisfied.

"Don't forget the sugar," said the man next to him. "It's the most important thing of all."

That was news to Chris. The soldier explained that the roll contained pure dextrose. It was quickly absorbed into the bloodstream and gave you energy. Energy is what they

64

would need for covering the last stretch to the camp.

Before they moved on, Chris saw a radio transmitter in use. It was not big—just a little box with a handle. Several meters of aerial could be pulled out of it. A pointer, a wavelength dial, and several knobs and switches were on one side of it.

"A walkie-talkie," said the soldier as he patted the box affectionately, "a soldier's best friend."

He spoke into an ordinary telephone receiver.

"Golden Arrow calling Panther Two, over. Golden Arrow calling Panther Two, over."

The connection came through. Chris did not understand much of the conversation as he could not hear the other party. He did understand that they had to be in camp within two hours. He was beginning to feel stiff and cramped from sitting and was glad when the signal to move on was given.

The last lap of the march was not pleasant. It was dark, and an icy wind began to blow. The dextrose did give them energy, but it could not keep the cold out. Chris was frozen, and his eyes smarted from lack of sleep. His hand ached. It was poor comfort knowing that the brakeman was worse off. He fell constantly, and he swore the Germans to damnation each time Chris helped him up onto his feet again.

Never had Chris lived through two longer hours. His legs were like lead, his heart hammered in his throat, and he had a cloying sweet taste in his mouth.

Suddenly he saw light up ahead. Great bonfires were burning, and he heard the roar of several planes in the sky. They were heavy cargo planes, not fighters, and the roar of their engines mounted to thunder. They were directly overhead. As the moon broke through a cloud, Chris noticed that the sky was full of parachutes. There were no men under them but large containers.

They were out in the middle of a frozen lake, a little apart from the others. Chris had no idea where Bent was, but the brakeman stood some distance apart and stared at the sky. Chris saw several men come running. The soldier with the tired eyes, who had led their party, was among them.

One of the chutes had not unfolded, and the heavy container rammed into the brakeman before he could move.

There was only a black hole left in the ice.

The soldier with the tired eyes had not seen this.

"Well done," he shouted excitedly. "Let's get the stuff inside."

8

IT was evening when Chris awoke. He felt stiff and sore all over, and the hand he had so foolishly injured on the train was bandaged so tightly that he could hardly move it. He remembered how the brakeman had met his death on the ice but not how he had ended up in this bed.

He looked around at the long, narrow room. There was a door on his right and seven beds besides his own. The two men from the engine were there, both fast asleep. All the beds were lined up along one wall. Along the other, there were stools and tables with glasses, thermometers, bandages, and bedpans. The room had two windows.

There were several soldiers outside, waving their arms wildly. Something must have happened.

The door opened, and Bent came in. He was pale.

"How are you, Chris," he said.

"I'm fine, Bent, but what's going on?"

"The Nazis. They have started taking hostages. The news was broadcast from London this afternoon. They shot ten people in town, chance passersby. They stopped a streetcar on the square and ordered everyone out. The first ten men were herded into a car, driven out to the Gestapo headquarters, and shot. There have been raids all over town."

Chris sat up in bed.

"The mad dogs!" he said heatedly. "That's like them!"

Bent sat down on the bed and took his brother's hand.

"Yes," he said quietly, "it is very like them, and they won't stop at that."

"It can't be long now." Anger flickered in his eyes. "They're getting panicky."

"That only makes them more desperate."

Suddenly Chris noticed that his brother was in a brown uniform and had a pistol in his belt.

"Man!" he exclaimed in deep admiration.

"It took a while for you to notice." Bent straightened proudly.

"Tell me all about it, but first about last night."

"There isn't much to tell about last night. You just collapsed on the ice. Tom and I carried you in here. Have you ever heard of the Nordseter Mountain Hotel?"

Chris shook his head. Bent continued. "This is it. It was a popular winter sports resort before the war. Now it's an army camp. It has an operating theater, a first-aid clinic, and this infirmary. The doctor bandaged you up; we undressed you and put you to bed without waking you. You should see the blisters on your feet."

"I don't care about the blisters." Chris snapped impatiently. "Did you say army camp?"

"Right. The entire mountain is a military base called Panther. This is Panther Two. Panther One, the headquarters, is deeper in the mountains, around Langestoel. All recruits are enrolled here. They get a medical examination, are equipped with uniforms and weapons, and are given their basic military training."

"The real military?" Chris said unbelievingly.

"As military as it can be."

"And the Germans don't know?"

"It won't be long now before they find out."

"How many are we?"

"*We* are many." A slight smile flitted across Bent's face. "At least a hundred, and there are even more at headquarters. Most of them are camped in cottages around here. Only the officers and the new recruits have their quarters in this building—and of course the Sparks, the radio operator. Funny, isn't it—he was my physics teacher at school."

Chris was no longer listening.

"I want to get up."

He threw aside the blankets and swung his legs out of bed. His brother caught him just before he toppled over.

"Good heavens, I'm stiff as a poker."

He tried to smile at his helplessness, but it was a rather crooked smile. Bent laughed in a friendly way.

"If it's any help, I was in exactly the same fix. All you need is a rubdown."

"Then give me one!"

Chris rolled back into bed and angrily stuck his legs out.

"Easy now." Bent was firm. "You'll wake the others."

There seemed to be no danger of that. The two railwaymen were sleeping heavily. Sometimes they grunted faintly. Empty plates stood on their bedside tables. All of a sudden Chris was ravenously hungry.

"Hurry up!" he said. "You still haven't told me how you got your uniform. Ouch!"

Bent had begun to massage the calf of Chris's leg and seemed to be doing his best to mash it.

"It wasn't easy," he said gravely.

"What do you mean by that?"

"I mean they are hunting a traitor. Every building around the submarine base was blown to bits. Every one of our men who fired the rowboats that were supposed to mark the targets has been arrested. Only Tom and I escaped. London ordered us out here so that we could be questioned."

"Are you under suspicion then?" Chris was sick with fear.

"Who knows!" His brother's expression was troubled. "They enrolled us all right, but we were questioned separately."

"What did they want to know?"

"Everything, but mostly what happened on the promontory. They couldn't understand why the Germans let us blow up the oil tanks. How could I answer? I don't understand it either."

"Have you spoken to Tom?"

"Yes."

"What did he say?"

"Not much. He was sullen."

"He almost always is."

70

"Yes, often, and I don't know why."

Chris sat pondering for a while. "If it were up to me," he said, "I wouldn't accept Tom's explanations point blank."

"They do sound strange." His brother hesitated. "But mine don't sound any better."

"Maybe they know more than you think."

"Let's hope so."

It had grown dark. Bent switched on the light.

"This place has its own power station," he explained.

Two naked bulbs lit the room dimly. Loud voices and the tramp of boots could be heard outside. It sounded like a noisy class of school children. Bent went to see what was happening.

Once alone, Chris made a new effort to stand up. This time with more success. He was hard on himself and angry because he had let the long trek on skis get the better of him. He was upset by his brother's despondency. After all, they were now free men in an unoccupied part of Norway—or was that just something they imagined? He refused to think along such lines. Things had worked out, hadn't they, and as soon as he was on his feet again, they would be like the three musketeers. He had just given up trying to get his boots on when Bent returned, looking disturbed.

"Well?"

"The Nazis are killing people indiscriminately. Some of our men from the little town where we got the extra engine just came in. They left there early this morning. By then the Nazis had already shot twelve people. The station-master was the first to be killed. They have been arresting people wildly all evening. The town is in a panic."

"Why doesn't anyone give them a fight?"

"Are you crazy, Chris?" His brother's anxiety had given way to dismay. "The underground acts only on orders from London."

"Did you and Father act on orders, too?"

"That was different—in fact, it was foolish."

"You didn't have to say that."

"I guess you are old enough to know."

"It cost Father his life."

"And what has it cost me?"

"Yes, Bent, what has it cost you?"

Chris repeated the question as he stared hard at his brother. Bent evaded his gaze and, instead of answering the question, put his arms around Chris.

"Oh, Chris, what have they done to you?"

Chris pulled away. He felt uncertain and a little ashamed.

"Nobody has done anything to me," he said, flustered, "and nobody ever will."

"You're wrong, Chris. What happened to me is now happening to you."

Chris did not see the kindness in his brother's eyes, just the concern, which he mistook for cowardice. He felt confused. He knew he had said something wrong but not why it was wrong. He grew angry and wanted to hurt Bent.

"I guess I was wrong about you," he said as he pulled his ski socks over the bandages. He slammed the door hard as he walked out and regretted having done so even before he heard the bang.

A lot of men were sitting in the living room at the end of the corridor. The smoke was so thick that Chris could hardly make them all out. Everyone seemed excited. The leader of the long trek was among them. He was steely-eyed, but he no longer looked so tired.

"There's our colt," he yelled the minute he caught sight of Chris. "Come and meet the boys."

Chris nodded left and right; they thumped him on the back and slapped his shoulder until he was befuddled.

"Call me Bas," said the leader as he shook Chris's hand.

"I thought a 'bas' was foreman of the crew." Chris was outspoken.

"Right on the nose, Colt. I'm foreman of a dynamiting crew."

Everyone laughed; then suddenly someone yelled, "Quiet!" It was time for the evening news broadcast from London. The day was Thursday, the twenty-sixth of April, and the announcer's brisk voice filled the room.

"There are no more chinks in the iron ring the Russians have thrown around Berlin. Fierce fighting is going on in the sewers and the subways. All males between the age of fifteen and sixty-five have been conscripted for the defense of Berlin. Twelve-year-old boy volunteers are trying to ward off the advancing Russian tanks. Entire classes of schoolboys and their teachers are fighting side by side in the burning city. . . ." Chris listened, impressed, and could not quite understand why the news seemed to embitter the soldiers.

In referring to Norway, the speaker didn't say anything about recent executions but only that the mass arrests continued. A dry announcement about the heavy bombing of a new German airstrip in the early hours of the morning caused a rustle of pleased excitement among the listeners.

"That explains why no reconnaissance planes have been around," Bas said contentedly. "Let's see if he has anything for us in his bag of goodies."

The announcer did. The "bag of goodies" were special announcements following the ordinary newscasts, and Chris listened with increasing wonder to the weird jumble of sentences that came through.

"Moonlight and rain. Grandfather is asleep tonight. Flowers in the wilderness. The horse is without a rider. The cat is under the oven."

The message they were waiting for was "blueberries and red currant jelly." It was received enthusiastically. It meant more supplies would be air-dropped around midnight.

"And then we'll be able to give the Germans a warm welcome," said Bas to Chris.

It was time to eat. The dining room was in the other end of the lodge. Most of the men Chris had met did not live in the building but in cottages outside. There were almost twenty men at the table. Bent and Tom sat beside each other, but Chris noticed that they hardly said a word to one another throughout the meal.

They had bacon for supper, and Chris helped himself as if he had never learned table manners. The meal was thoroughly satisfying. He sat beside the two newcomers, and from their conversation he gathered that the stationmaster in charge of the station where the extra engine had been secured had not known that the military transport was to be sabotaged. The underground had put on two of their own men from the private railroad lines because the regular crew was not reliable. So Tom had been right.

The Germans soon realized that all was not well, and when the motorized handcars that had been sent on reconnaissance returned with the terrible truth, the commandant had gone into a frenzy. The stationmaster was shot in his own office. The men were sorry about that. He had been a good Norwegian.

"That's war!" Chris blurted out.

They stared at him in surprise but said nothing.

After supper Chris was ordered back to bed by the doctor.

The doctor was a funny kind of fellow with a turned-up nose and a thatch of red hair. Everyone called him "Red," he said. He told Chris that, although he lived less than five kilometers from the camp, he had not seen his wife in two years. Within that period of time, he had been trained in England as a commando. He and Bas had bailed out over the mountains and parachuted down. At first they had had to haul all supplies from the landing spots along the coast up into the mountains. Each trip could take several days. It had been rough. Now all supplies were air-dropped directly, and, by comparison, it was child's play to be a soldier behind the enemy lines. The drop they were waiting for would be mostly uniforms and provisions. They expected a large-scale attack after the recent events in town.

Red guaranteed that Chris would be able to get into his boots the next day. Until then, he would have to make do with a pair of old carpet slippers. Chris was more than satis-

75

fied with the guarantee and decided to go exploring before he went to bed. He got no farther than the radio room.

It was a little room without windows on the second floor. There was a large table full of radio apparatus. The Sparks sat with his back to the door and spoke into a microphone.

"Panther Two calling Outstation Five, Panther Two calling Outstation Five. Over to you, over."

The Sparks repeated the call several times. Finally he threw the microphone down on the table.

"They're all snoring away, of course," he said crossly, "and we're supposed to run a war with those sluggards." Then he turned toward Chris and said, "I expect you are our boy soldier."

Chris liked that kind of talk. "Yes," he said. "I shall probably get my uniform tomorrow."

The Sparks laughed. "Yes, you probably will."

Chris was not aware of his gentle irony.

"What's going on?" Chris asked.

"Nothing, I'm just sitting here calling in the outposts for the air drop. We're expecting about twenty planes, and we'll need all the hands we can get."

The Sparks told him that Panther Two had eight outposts with between eight and ten soldiers in each. They were to listen in for the instructions from London and keep in touch with the lodge regularly. Occasionally they were so busy with outdoor combat training that they forgot. That could hardly be the explanation now. "I imagine they are on their way here already."

Chris was not particularly interested in the soldiers at the moment. He wanted to know how the planes found the camp. It sounded easy enough when the Sparks explained. When the planes were heard approaching, two red and two white lights were switched on in an L pattern at the site of the air drop—red, white, red showing the direction of the wind, and the second white light a little apart, turned against the wind.

If the moon was not out, they lit ground flares and used a direction finder. The direction finder sent out signals that were received by a similar device on the plane. When the plane had its bearings, it sent signals to the ground crew to light the flares. The Sparks asked Chris if he understood.

Chris had understood.

"Don't things ever go wrong?" he asked.

"You saw how wrong yesterday evening. It's impossible to rule out such accidents. When the wind gets at the containers, it sometimes pushes them off course. No use trying to run. It's best just to stand and hope for the best. Did you know him?"

"No, but I liked him," answered Chris, thinking of the brakeman.

"Take care not to make friends at this camp. It only makes it rougher if anything should happen, and something will happen very soon. The Germans know we're here, but not exactly where. The wind has carried containers beyond the mountain plateau and down into the valley, where the Germans have found them. They haven't done anything about it yet because we have kept quiet. The blowing-up of the mountain railway was our first mission. We'll not have to wait long before they get here."

Chris nodded. The Sparks was an exciting man to know.

He was big and strong and suntanned. He was probably much older than Bas. Chris could not imagine him sitting at a teacher's desk. "Bent, tell us about Archimedes' principle."

He must remember to ask Bent what kind of teacher the Sparks had been. Lots of fun, no doubt. Nothing with chemical formulas, magnets, or litmus paper, just fun. He had to get hold of Bent.

One of the radio devices started clacking. It was a receiver. A white ribbon of paper snaked slowly over the table.

The Sparks examined it closely. "It's London," he said. "I'll have my hands full. You had better run along. The planes will be here any minute."

The lodge was almost empty when Chris got downstairs. There were a few stragglers on their way out, but Bent was not among them.

From the doorway Chris could see the signal lights a couple of hundred meters away. There were soldiers swarming all over the place. It was a clear, moonlit night, but you could see a storm was brewing in the north. The planes came in low over the plateau. There must have been more than twenty—thirty perhaps—but some flew further on. The roar of the engines was infernal. The windowpanes rattled, and Chris's ears filled with thunder. He ducked instinctively as the heavy planes whipped over the lodge with open bomb doors. The heavy containers trailed out like corn out of a sack, the chutes opened with a snap, and soon the sky was studded with colored umbrellas distinguishable in the moonlight—some light, some dark. They swayed down to the ground. Some of the parachutes did not open, and the containers came hurtling down to the ground, sending plumes of snow high into the air as they landed.

It was all over in less than a minute, and even before the roar of the last plane had died away, soldiers came back, dragging the first container behind them. It had started to snow.

"Just what we need!" said the Sparks, who was standing behind Chris with a piece of paper in his hand. "Have you seen Bas?"

Chris shook his head. "Bad news?"

"That depends on how one feels. Two fjord boats full of Germans sailed from town this afternoon. It looks as if they are on their way here."

The moon was no longer visible. The mountain plateau was shrouded in darkness. From the north, the wind started blowing in sudden gusts.

9

CHRIS had never imagined he would long for a mirror the way he did that morning in the supplies depot. A full-length mirror, the kind tailors use—preferably new and shiny. He would stand in front of it, click his heels together, and salute smartly.

"Private 203 reporting for duty!"

Wouldn't that be the day! For the present he had to make do with a hand mirror, but he managed to get the beret with Royal Ensign into the reflection.

He was wearing the King's uniform, and it was only nine o'clock in the morning of the second day at the camp.

The last two hours had been eventful. Bent had awakened him around seven. He was sitting on the bed next to Chris.

"Hey, Chris, we have to get up."

Chris looked at Bent sleepily and understood that all was to be forgotten. There was nothing to talk about and nothing to remember. He admired his brother more than ever.

The infirmary was full. Tom was there, too. He was in the process of pulling his shirt over his head.

"We have hard work ahead of us," said Bent. "We found no more than half the containers last night, and by now they are probably buried in enormous snowdrifts."

Chris was in too much of a hurry to wait for Red. He took off the bandages and covered his blisters with Band-Aids he had found on a table with first-aid equipment. Then he got his boots on quite easily. There was no time to be wasted in a sick bed. The mountain lodge was alive with people, mostly new. They had arrived during the night. It was easy to tell them apart from the others. They had no uniforms, and their faces were grimy and lined with fatigue. Chris felt quite the veteran as he showed one of them the way to the toilet.

The radio was going full blast in the living room, but he caught only short snatches of the broadcast as he stuffed himself with oatmeal and condensed milk.

"Russian troops are battling in the streets of Berlin to reach the ring of defense around Hitler's headquarters. All troops along the Elbe front have been ordered to the German capital—Berlin is on fire after a heavy Allied bombing."

Everyone looked grave when Chris came into the living room. Bas said, "No news from the town this time either. That can only mean bad news. They must have unraveled the organization. The devil take them! They must have known more than we imagined."

Red did not agree. "I don't think so. All that has happened looks too damn much like the work of a traitor."

Chris felt uncomfortable, and he was about to leave when one of the officers said, "Follow me, Colt."

He seemed nice enough, but he wasn't much of a talker.

"This way."

He opened the door at the end of the corridor. In the room there was a desk and a shelf full of office folders. He sat at the table.

"You have to be registered," he said with a faint smile. He then asked Chris a lot of questions. His date of birth, address, and the names of his relatives. Finally he said Chris was now Private 203 of the Free Norwegian Forces.

"We have been talking about you," he continued, "and have decided that it is safer to register you as a soldier. If things go wrong, you will be treated as a prisoner of war instead of being shot as a partisan. But if we ever catch you near a weapon, we will lock you up for the rest of the war. Don't forget for one single second that you are a boy!"

Chris nodded. He could afford to swallow the insults. He was a soldier now, and everything else would work out.

The lieutenant, for that was his rank, easily seen by the number of stripes on his sleeve, got up and said he would take Chris to Candy Peter.

Candy Peter was the supplies officer. Chris was better able to understand his strange nickname when he got into the depot. There were shelves full of chocolate, candy, and cookies, and, of course, military supplies—boots, ski underwear, pants, jackets, and sweaters, knitted caps, and camouflage suits.

Chris was equipped completely. He had to help himself because Candy Peter was busy putting away the things from the containers the soldiers brought in. Everything was in a mess, but Chris felt it was the most promising mess he had ever seen.

"Can't I help?" he offered generously as he put down the mirror.

"Some other time, Colt." Candy Peter's voice was friendly. "Get out in the sun. You need it."

It was warm in the sun. Outside, a large group of soldiers was emptying the containers, and others came dragging more they had dug out of the snow.

Chris found himself a pair of skis. He wanted to get out there and find Bent.

A fresh wind was blowing, and he saw the soldiers struggling with the parachutes each time the wind got hold of them. He found Bent standing on a ridge a good distance away from the lodge. Here the wind had free play. The snow lay in heavy drifts in some spots, and in others it was hard polished ice. A container stood hammered halfway down in the ice. It was crumpled like an accordion, and the contents lay strewn about. It was quite a sight: marmalade, canned food, cookies, chocolate, butter, sausages—and corned beef. Bent walked around collecting the remains in a sack.

"You can take care of that container over there," he shouted.

Chris had to look for a while before he found it. The bottom of the upside-down container was barely visible in a huge snowdrift. He took his skis off and used one of them as a shovel. It worked quite well, and before long he had the container dug out. It was much worse trying to dig out the parachute as it lay under piles of closely packed snow. Finally he succeeded and was undoing the cords when a sudden gust of wind filled the parachute like a sail. Before Chris knew it, he was sitting astride the container launched on a reckless ride down the icy slope. He shot away. The snow whirled up in high sprays on either side. He dared not let go, but at the same time it was fun. The parachute carried him up snowdrifts, out into space, and down once more.

"Ahoy," he yelled at the openmouthed soldiers as he sped by. "Ahoy!"

What a ride for Private 203!

Crash!

The container slammed into an enormous snowdrift and cut deep into it—with Chris still on top. There he was, lodged in the heavy snow like a human bullet.

They came running from all directions. Was he hurt? Of course not! Would he consider flying all the other containers to the lodge? Would he! Well, he was a little dazed, but the transportation to the foot of the lodge was quick.

Red came and felt his arms and legs. He was in one piece. A miracle!

"Your nose is bleeding. Get in and wash your face, and no more pranks today, if you please!"

He really was bleeding! It irritated him to see the blood dribbling onto his new uniform. Perhaps he was a little dizzy. There was Bent.

"You crazy goon!"

"I'm all right!"

"Come along then!"

His nose stopped bleeding. Chris's face was rinsed and dried in the first-aid room. Gradually he realized how lucky he had been. The ice crystals could have sliced him up badly. He must have held his mittened hands in front of his face. He was not quite sure whether he should feel ashamed or not. After all, it had not been his fault that the parachute suddenly went wild. He knew he should have jumped off in time. He decided to behave as if nothing had happened, like a soldier.

There was heavy traffic on the slopes when Chris came out again. The soldiers were riding their valuable cargoes in with parachutes billowing.

"Thanks for the idea, Colt," one of them yelled as he stopped the big container at the lodge in a cloud of powdery snow.

Chris blushed with pride. He didn't need to be ashamed of anything. Shots from the lake where he had seen his first container gave him something else to think about. They were having shooting practice. He hurriedly fastened his skis and sped away.

New recruits were being instructed. Among them was Bent, holding an English machine gun. Chris had heard the soldiers call it a Sten gun. Bent stood with his legs wide apart and the gun held across his body. He looked great! Chris was proud of his brother and hardly envied him at all. The instructor exercised them unrelentingly. They ran and fired; they threw themselves in the snow and fired; they kneeled and fired. They worked with skis and without skis.

He could not understand why the instructor ordered him to leave. He was a big fellow with ugly eyes.

"Get lost, Colt," he said harshly.

Chris looked down his bloodstained coverall. After all, wasn't he a soldier?

"Listen here," he began.

"No, you listen." The instructor's voice was flat and humorless. "We're ready to start commando training. We don't want you to practice silent killing when you get back to school!"

Chris made no reply. He turned on his heel and walked towards the air-drop zone.

"Remember, Colt," the instructor shouted out after him, "a soldier never questions an order."

He might have known it. Chris was good and mad. When would he ever get a chance like this again? He was not sure he liked being called Colt any more.

No one was at the dropping area. The last of the drums were being emptied at the lodge.

At lunch, Chris sat beside a funny little fellow with hardly any hair on his head and an expression on his face that showed no distaste for another meal of corned beef. He must have been very hungry because he had not bothered to take off his gun belt and to put his rucksack beside him.

"I've heard about you," he said between two mouthfuls. "We must get together and talk. What's your name?"

Chris told him and added, "They call me Colt."

"Don't let that bother you. They call *me* Mr. All-in-One." He laughed heartily, and when Chris stared at him in surprise, he leaned over and whispered confidingly, "It's because of this." He patted the rucksack with affection. "I always have it with me. Everything I need is in it; the chalice, the altar cloth, the prayer book, the Bible, and the hand grenade."

Chris kept on staring at him. "Do you mean," he stammered, "do you mean you're the minister?"

"Right. You see, there is nothing like a hand grenade in

86

close combat, but you have to keep yourself covered. Well, you'll learn all about that."

Mr. All-in-One resumed his interrupted meal. Chris was a little puzzled but decided to try the food instead.

He watched for Bent during the meal. His brother came in with the others from the training area. He had to get hold of Bent and ask him all about the Sten gun. In return he would tell him a thing or two about using hand grenades in close combat.

The minister with the curious baggage interrupted his thoughts. "Let's take a walk," he said as they left the table. "You must tell me all about yourself, and I will tell you all you need to know about us crackpots."

The wind had stopped blowing, and the sun shone warmly out of a clear sky. Red joined them out on the steps. He was in a bad mood.

"You just don't know how well off you are among us black souls, All-in-One," he snapped. "Next time I see a festering blister, I'll vomit."

"I gather you haven't heard the latest news," the minister replied.

"All the news I have is that I'm running out of cod-liver-oil ointment."

"We've lost track of the Germans in the boats."

"The hell you say!"

"Even worse. They are Alpine troops."

"But do you think they . . ." Red paused. "They couldn't."

"We've said that before about those . . ."

"Devils!" Red finished the sentence.

"Thank you," said Mr. All-in-One vaguely.

Chris had listened to their conversation without understanding any of it. They started to explain the situation to him, but so eagerly that they interrupted each other.

There was only one obvious route to the mountain lodge: a path from the west along the edge of the plateau. It wound its way up from the village. It was steep but accessible even in winter. Panther Two had outposts strung out along this path and well-fortified positions at the end, which could be manned within minutes.

The other possible route crossed the mountains from the south, the way they had gone after sabotaging the train. But using this route required exact knowledge of the location of the camp. Otherwise, it was like looking for a grain of sand in the Sahara. Panther One lay across the mountains to the east.

In the north, cliffs rose sheerly from the sea to giddying heights. They had never come up this way, even in an emergency. Alpine troops could only mean that the Germans were planning to attack from the north.

"I guess an avalanche is too much to hope for," said Red.

"It is." The minister smiled. "At least as long as we don't know exactly where they'll come from."

"Why don't we send out scouting patrols?" Chris asked.

He hadn't had a chance to study the contour of the mountains. He now looked at them carefully and shuddered. They were hideous mountains, ugly warts that even the snow couldn't soften. Frequent avalanches disfigured their icy slopes, leaving greenish-black scars shining in the sun. The tops were hidden in a swirl of snow.

Mr. All-in-One looked at him. "I see you have guessed the answer," he said. "We don't have enough men to comb so vast an area, and it really isn't necessary. Bas has a plan that will lure the enemy straight to us. The success of the plan depends on the Nazis not knowing how many we are. We can safely assume that they do not, or else they would have been here by now. When they discover the mountain lodge—and we will make sure they don't miss it—they will launch an attack here at the lower end of the plateau. We are to defend ourselves, of course, but most of the work will be done by the men from the outposts. As soon as the enemy has been located, they will be surrounded and ambushed."

"They won't have the chance of a snowball in hell," said Red approvingly. "Now I see why the boys were in such a hurry."

"They have to be rested. They didn't get much sleep last night, and they have a tough job ahead of them."

"So do I." Red was grave. "I'd better get back and clean up the place."

"You have plenty of time. They won't get here until sometime tomorrow at the earliest. Let's listen to what our friend Colt has to say."

They were almost at the edge of the plateau. The ground was uneven, and boulders big as houses blocked the view. They found a good spot for sunning themselves and stopped to rest. The two men lit their pipes and nodded encouragingly.

Chris did not feel as if he had much to tell after all the exciting things he had heard. Orders were orders, however. He began with that terrible day in the library, and as it all came back to mind, his father's face in death was no longer ugly, nor was it beautiful. Yet he could not forget the sight. He kept on talking about his father's face.

"You loved your father?" Mr. All-in-One interrupted.

"Yes," Chris answered from far away.

"You hate the Nazis, don't you?"

"Yes, I hate them." Chris smiled, but his eyes were expressionless. "I hate them!"

"Listen, Colt"—the minister put his arm around the boy —"listen, my friend. You must be wondering what I—a man of the Church—am doing here among soldiers."

"No."

"All right then. But let me tell you this. War is hate and God is love. Hate kills more of us than war."

Chris looked confused.

"Listen to him, Colt, he's right," said Red. "Now who the devil is that?"

A man had appeared from behind the boulders some fifty meters away. The man was wearing a ski suit. He waved at them.

The minister said, "He's not one of our men."

Red stepped forward. "I'd better take a closer look."

Chris saw the flash and heard the shot, but at the same moment he was hurled to the ground. Mr. All-in-One had pulled Chris down with him.

"Lie still!" he hissed.

A little distance from them Red lay with his head twisted unnaturally in their direction. There was a hole in his forehead, and blood trickled from it. A machine gun started spluttering. The bullets kicked up the snow around them.

90

10

CHRIS had pushed his head so far down in the snow that he could hardly breathe. He heard one explosion and then another. And a curse: "Evil shall be driven out with evil!"

"Mr. All-in-One!" Chris called.

"Everything's all right. Crawl backward and get behind that boulder."

A new round of machine-gun fire began. The bullets ripped into the boulder with a frightening sound. Mr. All-in-One's pistol hammered back.

"Now!"

There was a terrible authority in that one word, which frightened Chris more than the firing. But he was stuck in the snow. It had piled up behind him like a wall, so he couldn't move. He made a gigantic effort, half lifted himself, and crawled to cover behind the boulder they had used as a back rest.

Mr. All-in-One followed. He crept backward, pulling his rucksack after him as a shield for his head. Once in safety he swung the rucksack high above his head. His eyes were fierce.

"There, we cheated them!"

The bullets had nearly cut the rucksack in two. Mr. All-in-One shook out the contents. The chalice was as misshapen as a squashed orange. Mr. All-in-One smiled grimly.

"A good thing that rat didn't hit this," he said as he looked at the hand grenade he was holding, "because now is the time to use it."

No more shots were fired. Mr. All-in-One loaded his pistol as he mumbled, "If only I could get behind him . . ." He never finished the sentence. Shouts came from the lodge, and machine-gun bullets tore up the ground in front of them.

"Bas, the numbskull, he's finally caught on!"

Mr. All-in-One drew Chris closer to the boulder.

"This time we have to watch out for richocheting bullets. What a weapon, that Bren gun!"

The salvos swept over the plateau.

Mr. All-in-One signaled with his pistol and cursed the guards roundly for not being at their posts. "Sunning themselves, as usual!"

There were many men in front of the lodge. Even at a distance Chris could see they were getting ready to take off. Then everything happened all at once.

From behind a boulder a new figure appeared, again a man in a ski suit. He waved a handkerchief wildly as he ran toward them. Then Chris saw that the man who had shot Red lay still in the snow a short distance from them. The other man bent over him. A machine gun crackled from behind the boulder, and the man crumpled over into the snow.

Mr. All-in-One was gone. Chris spotted him behind another boulder with his pistol in one hand and his hand grenade in the other. He shouted something. A third man in a ski suit was creeping forward slowly, too slowly. Mr. All-in-One shot him.

Chris ran over to Mr. All-in-One. Two of their own men crawled out from behind the boulder.

"They took us by surprise. God knows where they came from," they said.

Mr. All-in-One said nothing. His face was pale as he stuffed the grenade into his pocket.

"Let's take a look at them," he said shortly.

Now the guards started talking. "The Germans—those men spoke German—had a radio transmitter with them. The receiver cannot be far away. We understood that much."

The transmitter was standing in the snow with the receiver off the hook. Mr. All-in-One lifted the receiver and shouted, *"Ende!"*

He then fired his pistol at it until no more bullets were left. They shattered the wooden container into a pile of shavings.

"Get inside!" Mr. All-in-One said to Chris.

"Get back to your posts!" he said to the guards.

He walked over to Red and carried him into the shelter of a boulder.

He overtook Chris halfway up to the lodge. All the others were there, too. They had come rushing out as soon as the shooting had stopped. Before anyone could say anything, bullets began to rain down on them.

Many fell, there and then. Chris clung to Mr. All-in-One. The battle in the mountains had begun.

Bullets sang in the air and hit their targets with a grotesque sound. He saw a man die, a giant of a man with a huge head of black curly hair. The bullets literally yanked him out of the snow and pitched him forward as if a great fist had struck him. It was weirdly funny to see him sail headfirst into the snow. Several of the men laughed. Chris snickered.

Mr. All-in-One crouched with his hand grenade in one hand and his pistol in the other. The weapons looked ridiculous at a time like this. The firing was coming from far up the mountainside.

The man with the black curly hair screamed that he was dying. Chris thought, "A man, afraid to die?"

Just then he heard Mr. All-in-One's prayer, "Be with this man in his time of need, Almighty God. Ease his suffering and free his soul from fear."

But the screams continued, and Chris realized that others had been hit. Some yelled, some whimpered, and others swore.

A heavy and persistent barrage of gunfire sounded from the lodge. The rest of the Bren guns must have been mounted. Chris didn't dare lift his head to look, but he was sure Bent was behind one of the machine guns. The spray of bullets from above was thinning out the group of men on the plateau. They must have been as easy to pick off as sitting ducks.

The shooting from the mountain petered out as the firing from the lodge became more emphatic.

"Let's take cover under the ledge," Mr. All-in-One said hoarsely.

It was the skimpiest ledge Chris had ever seen. It was almost nothing but a small rise in the ground, but it could afford them some cover. Chris started crawling with Mr. All-in-One close behind. Several of the men followed. Some groaned. Chris wished they would be quiet.

It was a long way to crawl. Chris thought they would never get there. Not being able to see what was going on seemed unbearable.

The last stretch was easy enough. They had only to crawl between the snowdrifts around the house. Then they made a dash for the steps. Enemy bullets tore into the end wall of the lodge; they splintered the skis outside and shattered the windows. The rest got in without injuries.

Inside, everything was chaos. The men were shooting from the windows or from holes they had hacked through the walls. They swore and shouted obscenities at one another. Chris had never heard such words, and he listened eagerly.

Most of all he listened to the orders. "Three Sten guns to the corner room, one Bren gun at the bay window." The orders continued to fly.

"Where the hell are the medics?" Two men in the front room are making a fuss. "Where the hell is Red?"

Men hurried past him. One took him by the scruff of the neck and roared, "Get out of the way, boy!" It was Bas. He did not wait for protest; he just threw him down the corridor. Chris landed at the foot of the stairs exactly at the moment they were yelling for the Sparks.

"I'll find him," Chris thought. He dashed up the stairs and almost bumped into a limp body hanging over the banister at the landing.

The radio room and the Sparks were barely recognizable. One entire wall had been shot full of holes. He could see the mountainside through them. The table and radio apparatus were not much damaged. The Sparks stood bent over them. His face and hands were bleeding, and his uniform was soaked in blood.

Chris, too, was covered with blood. His coverall was torn, and his hands were sticky. Discovering this made him feel dizzy.

The Sparks juggled with the apparatus and called, "Panther Two calling Outstation Five. Over. Panther Two calling . . . At last! Where the devil have you been? Over. . . . You guessed right. All hell's loose. Operation B is to be launched immediately. . . . Will we make it? Looks bad. End of message."

The Sparks brought his hand down hard on the table and stood up. "Idiots," he mumbled.

Then he caught sight of Chris. "What in heaven has happened to you? Are you hurt?"

Chris was on the verge of tears. He shook his head. "There's a man hanging over the banister," he stammered. "I think he's dead."

"More than likely," said the Sparks, "and what are you doing here?"

"They have been asking for you."

"I bet they have. One of the outposts does not answer our call, but they must be on their way now. They had better hurry, or we'll be in the soup." He then gripped Chris firmly by the arm. "Come along. This is no place for you."

The soldier on the landing was gone, but the banister was smeared with blood. Chris shuddered. He looked at the banister and then at his hands. He felt sick and wished he could throw up. Not here, though, not in front of all the men. The Sparks held on to him firmly until he got all the way down the stairs. He told Chris to stay in the corridor while he looked for Bas.

The atmosphere was not so hectic as it had been, but the firing had become more intense. Chris was sneaking off to the toilet when one of the soldiers caught hold of him.

"You come with me!"

The man pushed him into the infirmary and told him to make himself useful.

There was blood everywhere. Chris felt the room start swaying. He grabbed the nearest bedpost and vomited noisily. Blushing with shame, he waited anxiously for derisive comments from the men. No comments were made. The men in the room had other matters to attend to.

Candy Peter stood in front of him. He was in his shirt sleeves. One of the men from the railway was trying to bind a scarf around his upper arm. The blood spurted out through the bandage.

Candy Peter swore hard and steadily. ". . . and that bastard of a doctor, too!"

The other railwayman was also putting on bandages. There were no other helpers. The wounded sat or lay on the beds. Some of them swore like Candy Peter. A couple lay quite still, and one moaned faintly. All of them had bloody bandages.

"What can I do?" Chris strained to make the words sound natural. He did not quite succeed.

The railwayman nearest him turned and gave him a haggard look. "Wash," he said flatly. "Wash!"

Chris was happy to get out of there. He went into the kitchen and found a bucket and a cloth. He filled the bucket with water. On the way back he tried looking for Bent, but he saw neither his brother nor Tom.

On his way out with the third bucket of water, he met the Sparks, who came charging in with encouraging news. "The outposts have taken their positions and will launch an attack any minute now."

The message was received with another stream of curses from the wounded.

Mr. All-in-One looked in, not to bring comfort but to make sure no one needed him.

"Just stray and ricocheting bullets," he said, and he gave Chris a friendly push with the hand that wasn't holding a machine gun. "Bad enough but not serious. It all happened within the first couple of minutes before we could tell where the firing came from."

Mr. All-in-One brought some news, too. Langestoel had been attacked by the enemy. "Luckily they were prepared."

"That bastard of a doctor," mumbled Candy Peter.

The minister looked at him severely. "Red didn't walk into a trap any more than you did," he said coldly, "nor did he have a wall between himself and the enemy."

"You know I didn't mean it that way," Candy Peter said, subdued.

"Then why don't you shut up!" answered Mr. All-in-One and left.

The firing from the lodge had almost stopped, but furious salvos sounded outside. Chris no longer felt sick. The battle was soon over. Chris found Bent and Tom in the front room. They stood talking with their weapons in hand. He

98

envied them their grown-up fellowship more than ever.

"Look at you!" Bent pointed at his brother's blood-stained coveralls in alarm.

"It's nothing." Chris glanced proudly down. "Did you get any of the Nazis?"

"I certainly hope so."

"Surely you must know."

"Not at that range."

"Did you see them?"

"Barely." His brother was dodging his questions.

"Our job was to keep them at a distance until the outposts came to our assistance," Tom explained.

Chris was not ready to quit. "How did it feel?"

"I think you should find yourself a new coverall while there are still some left." Bent gave him a gentle shove in the right direction.

It was a good suggestion because there was a crowd in the supplies depot. The battle had been short, but it had ruined many an outfit.

Candy Peter looked on helplessly as the soldiers raided his supplies. His arm was still not properly bandaged.

Chris got himself a brand-new set of clothes, but when he was about to filch a machine-gun shoulder strap, Candy Peter grabbed him with his good arm.

"You have to be able to crawl before you can run, my boy, and you be glad of that."

"I don't understand what you mean," answered Chris, annoyed with himself for not having understood.

"Take a look in the first-aid room—then perhaps you will understand," Candy Peter said.

Why not! Chris changed his clothes. He hadn't been inside the first-aid room yet. It was down the corridor. He opened the door and walked in. It was dark. He turned on the light. Two bodies lay on the floor. They were covered with blankets so that only the boots were visible. Did Candy Peter imagine he would be scared? He had seen his father stretched out on the floor without a blanket to cover his head. He was not afraid of death. He was just about to turn off the lights and leave when two soldiers carried Red in on a stretcher. Two more dead were brought in. The stretcher-bearers said that these last two were from the outposts. The outposts had lost only those two, and they had no injured men. The entire German contingent of forty-seven men had been wiped out.

Chris counted quickly. With the three scouts Mr. All-in-One had shot, it meant fifty dead Germans against five dead Norwegians. Not a bad result! Chris said so, but the men did not answer. They spread blankets over the bodies they had brought in and left. The last one turned to Chris.

"Do you plan to stay here?"

"No."

He had nothing more to do in the first-aid room, so he turned off the light and followed the soldier.

Chris asked, "How are things going at Langestoel?"

"The fight is over. We lost seven men."

"And the Germans?"

"Sixty-five."

That made the total twelve Norwegians against one hundred and fifteen Germans. Chris could not understand why the soldiers were not elated. Most of the men from the outposts had come in by now. There were soldiers standing and sitting everywhere. They ate corned beef and soup without complaining, as they discussed the battle in subdued voices.

The Germans must have found a new route up the east side of the mountain. Nothing else could explain why they had arrived twenty-four hours before they had been expected. They must also have known the position of the camp quite precisely. Treachery? They would never know. At least there was no doubt that the three men who took the guards by surprise were not only to divert attention but also to direct the attack with the help of the radio transmitter. The plan failed when Mr. All-in-One shot them.

It was time for the news broadcasts. The battle of Berlin was entering its last phase. The Allies had reached the ring of defense around Hitler's bunker. The Tiergarten was a sea of flame. Yet the German government was still broadcasting threats. ". . . a bottomless pit is yawning at the feet of The Third Reich. Germany will carry on."

The men around the radio stared at one another in amazement.

"They're crazy!"

There were no special messages for them. The Sparks came in a little later and handed Bas a piece of paper. Bas stood up.

"Get busy, boys. All forces are to retreat to Langestoel. We have to leave Nordseter before midnight."

He smiled at Chris on his way out. His face was as lined and anxious as on the first day.

11

A couple of hours later they were ready. Bonfires blazed along the horizon. The outposts had been set on fire. No supplies were to fall into the hands of the enemy. The men from the outposts had gathered together in front of the lodge. They had enormous packs on their backs.

They had had some busy hours at Nordseter. A burrow had been dug in the snow for the dead. They were to be fetched when everything was over. The wounded were wrapped in blankets and strapped onto sleds. Chris and Candy Peter watched mournfully as paraffin was poured over the food supplies. All the ammunition and weapons they could not carry were piled in the living room. A detonator was placed inside a package of plastic explosives, and a connecting wire was laid out all the way to the top of the ridge behind Nordseter. They all stood on the ridge, some hundred and fifty men, when Bas pushed down the plunger.

The explosion broke the quiet of the moonlit night. It was fantastic. It looked as if some tremendous force lifted the lodge and crumbled it into tiny pieces, which flew about like projectiles and hit the snow with sharp cracks.

Almost at the same moment flames shot up, and the remains of the lodge, where Chris had experienced the two most unusual days of his life, was a bonfire.

The trek began. A detachment including Bent and Tom, stayed behind to watch over the fire. Nothing was left to chance that night.

It was an endless procession. Chris was among those farthest behind and could not see the front of the line, even though the ground rose steeply. He walked beside Mr. All-in-One. The minister was silent and preoccupied. Chris did not dare to speak. He was a little afraid of Mr. All-in-One. The man had frightened Chris out there on the plateau. He had also saved his life. Chris knew he ought to thank him, but he could not find the words. Instead he ventured, "Why are we retreating?"

"Because it's necessary," Mr. All-in-One answered without looking at him.

"After all, we won!"

"Yes, we let them take us by surprise. They knew exactly where to find us."

"They have found Langestoel, too."

"That's different. The area is more suitable for defense. Nordseter was just a training camp and the starting point for minor operations, not a position of defense. Unless they use planes, and they can hardly spare fighter planes at this point, Langestoel is practically invulnerable."

"Then there is going to be some real fighting?" Chris was eager.

"I hope not."

Chris looked puzzled. Mr. All-in-One explained. "The big struggle is being decided somewhere else, my boy. The Nazis will surrender in a matter of days. I am not against sacrifice, but we don't have to go looking for trouble."

"What if we're attacked?"

"If we are attacked, we'll fight—fight hard. We're probably better equipped for mountain warfare than the Nazis. And we have more at stake."

The last bit cheered Chris up, and he pushed steadily on. Like the others, Chris carried a heavy pack. In his there were ten Bren gun magazine chambers. They were heavy. Chris could not remember ever having carried anything with greater pleasure. The blisters on his feet broke. In all the hurry he had forgotten to put on a fresh bandage. He clenched his teeth against the pain. In front of him Candy Peter moved forward with only one ski pole. His arm had finally been properly bandaged. He staggered and was no doubt dizzy from loss of blood.

The weather was still fine, but it got windy as they climbed higher, and the icy blasts slowed them down. Chris grew numb with cold, and he was very relieved when they reached their destination.

Langestoel was on top of a rather steep slope. It was a large building with a cluster of smaller cottages around it. Chris thought that it looked impressive in the cold, clear morning air. He was glad not to be attacking the place. There was a clear view of the surrounding country on all sides.

Although the day had hardly dawned, the headquarters

was humming with activity. Soldiers swarmed in and out of the cottages. Newcomers were hailed cheerfully, and old friends thumped one another on the back. Everyone was in good spirits.

The wounded were taken straight into the infirmary. Chris was among them. He could be brave no longer. The pain as he pulled his boot off brought tears to his eyes. The bandage was one blood-soaked rag. The medic looked from the sore to Chris with open admiration.

"Pretty brave, aren't you!"

With all his heart Chris wanted to say it was nothing, but he hadn't the strength to be brave any more.

They had their meals in the large building. Somehow they managed to make room for everyone at the table. There was soup and corned beef on the menu again, but the strange tension in the air from the evening before was gone. The two encounters were loudly discussed and commented upon. Chris was not listening. He did not listen to the morning news from London, which the others received with deafening applause, nor did he eat much. He felt quite sick.

He left the table, cleared a little spot under the stairway in the hall, rolled his blankets into a pillow for his head, and fell fast asleep.

It was day when he awoke. He was stiff from having slept on the hard floor. He was a little cold as well, but otherwise refreshed. He went outside and washed his face with snow. There was much activity between the cottages and headquarters. The air was alive with commands. The men were training and exercising. Nothing special was expected to happen, but the camp suddenly had to make room for twice as many soldiers as it was equipped to take. Chris enjoyed the commotion. This is just how he had imagined life in an army camp.

He was hungry and thirsty, and after some exploring, he found his way into the kitchen and asked for something to eat. The cook looked wild. He looked as if he had not slept for several days and was about to break down.

"Take it yourself."

There was coffee in a large pot and a dish with thick slices of corned beef. Chris began to understand why corned beef had a tendency to bring out the worst in the men, but it did not stop him from downing a sizable helping.

He went out to take a better look at the camp. Bas greeted him. He seemed to have found his happy face once more.

"Hi there, Colt!" he yelled. "Can you find your way around?"

"I manage." Chris liked Bas better and better. "When are the rest of the men due?"

"It can't be long now." Bas hurried on.

Chris could see there was a method in all the confusion. All the newcomers were practicing the use of arms. The instructor bawled them out roughly. Chris thought it was fun to listen. There was no end to the bawling out he could have taken had he been in their boots. He shrugged his shoulders. After all, the war was not over yet.

Machine-gun nests were being dug out on the slopes. Containers were hammered flat and wedged into the snow a foot apart. The hollow spaces were packed with snow, and water was poured over to make armored shields of ice.

Trenches led from the machine-gun nests to the large building. The snow lay so deep that the soldiers could walk upright to the basement door without being seen. There were even trenches from the cottages to the headquarters. Now they were ready for the Germans.

Chris had found a shovel and was ready to help when he caught sight of a group of soldiers on the slope below. That must be Bent and the others. He dropped the shovel and reached the detachment at about the same time Bas and Mr. All-in-One did. They spoke in low voices. Bent and Tom were missing.

He heard Bas say, "Then what happened?"

The leader of the detachment cleared his throat. "We were actually on our way, but one of the new fellows, Bent, had forgotten something and went back. He had nearly reached the ruins of the lodge when the shooting began. He fell almost at once. His friend fell just after."

Chris was chilled with fear. Bent shot! He was too shocked to say a single word.

The leader continued. "There were three of them, maybe survivors from the battle yesterday who had pretended to be dead. They must have been as surprised as we were, or they would hardly have opened fire. We got two of them. The third managed to escape."

Bas interrupted. "Were both our men killed?"

"Only Tom. He died immediately. We opened the burrow and put him in with the rest."

"What about Bent?"

"He was too badly hit to move. We built him a hut of boards we salvaged from the lodge and made him as comfortable as possible. We found a mattress that wasn't burned and several blankets. He won't be cold. He has a bucket of water and all our rations. And, of course, his Sten gun." The leader added, "It was hard leaving him. We had no choice. He's hit in the lung and won't last through the day."

Chris did not hear the last remark. He was on his way to the building with the ski sleds. Bent all alone in a hut of boards. Bent wounded, and the Germans would get there any minute. How could they leave him?

He pulled down one of the sleds, dragged it to the edge of the slope, threw himself upon it, and pushed away.

He did not hear the shouts behind him. He flew along. The ruts made by the sleds on the trek up were hard, and the sled practically steered itself. He needed all his strength just to hang on. He lay on his belly. Snow sprayed high on either side of him. The runners whined. In a flash he was on level ground. He grabbed the lead rope and staggered off to the next slope. Then it was downward once more. He had never gone sledding like this before, never felt his heart hammering this way, had never hated so much. They weren't going to take Bent away from him, too. He would get there first. It would not be long now.

The sled overturned. He went sprawling, and the ice crystals slashed his cheek open. He wiped his face with a handkerchief that turned red with blood. The sled had righted itself and gone, of course. He had to get past the deep snow. He staggered after the sled, and in some spots he sank in waist deep. He used all the obscenities he had heard the soldiers using. He scrambled after the sled until it crashed into a snowdrift and came to a standstill.

108

He tied the lead rope around his waist. There must be no more delaying accidents. He clung to the sled in another downhill dive.

How long had he been sledding—one hour, two hours, three hours? How many times had the sled overturned? How many times had he cried in pain and in rage? He did not know. When he saw the smoking ruins of the lodge below him, he forgot everything else. It was a horrible sight, and yet he was glad to see it, for this was where Bent had to be.

He did not find the hut right away. They had camouflaged it with snow. He found it when he was almost upon it. The opening was small, and it was dark inside.

Bent lay still with his eyes closed. He was covered up to the neck in blankets. Chris kicked out a board. More light came in, and he had a clearer view of the smoking ruins of the lodge and the plateau. No one would take them by surprise.

He sat beside his brother. Bent was very pale. He was breathing jerkily, and there was a bloody froth on his lips. Chris gently wiped it away.

"I'm here, Bent," he whispered.

His brother slowly opened his eyes. They were glazed, and his voice was barely audible.

"Chris."

"Yes, Bent. Everything will be all right."

His brother tried to smile, and the blood trickled out again.

"Chris," he repeated faintly.

"Please don't talk." Chris's eyes filled with tears.

109

"But there is something you must know, Chris."

"Later, Bent, when you feel stronger."

"It's about Tom, Chris." He tried to lift his head. Chris gently put his arm under his brother's neck.

"Are you thirsty?" he asked.

Bent nodded. There was a dipper in the bucket, and Chris lifted it carefully to his brother's lips. Bent was not able to swallow the water, but coughed it up with more blood.

"Listen . . . about Tom . . ." he said with great effort. "He was no traitor. He got killed trying to help me. He didn't have to die. Do you understand, Chris?"

Bent fell back exhausted and lay still with closed eyes. Chris couldn't think clearly. Tom was no traitor, but he was dead. Would Bent die, too?

Sharp commands in German sounded from far away. He saw them through the hole in the wall. They were at the edge of the plateau on the path that led up from the village. There were several of them, and they had horses and sleds with them.

"We must get out of here." Chris gave his brother's hand a gentle squeeze. "The Germans are coming. We must get back to camp. I have a ski sled."

Bent looked at him dully. His voice was weak. "I'm not going any place, but you are."

Chris looked silently at his brother's waxy face, and he accepted what he had known from the moment he had stepped into the hut. The leader had been right. Bent could not be moved. Anger welled up in him. He gripped the Sten gun at his brother's side. The safety catch was off.

"We won't surrender, Bent."

"Leave, Chris." There was dread in his brother's eyes. "Try not to think about what you've seen." Bent had raised himself halfway on his elbow. "You mustn't hate, Chris." His voice grew clear. "It's the worst thing that can happen to you. If you hate, you lose."

Chris was grimly watching the caravan move closer. There were three sleds full of soldiers and one with boxes and equipment. They pulled up in front of the ruins of the lodge. The soldiers got off and walked up to the smoking pile of rubble.

At that moment Chris opened fire. He kept his fingers pressed around the trigger and let showers of bullets sweep over the men and horses. He hit several of them. Men screamed. A horse reared. Then came the explosion. It was so violent that the hut was blown away.

The acrid smell of smoke smarted in his nostrils as Chris crawled out of the shambles. There was a gaping hole where the Germans had been. Horses and men lay strewn about in the snow.

He was paralyzed by the sight but only for a moment.

"I got them," he yelled as he began to dig his brother out. "I got them!"

Bent did not reply. His eyes were closed, and he did not move. Bent was dead.

Chris fell helplessly onto his knees beside his brother.

"I got them, Bent," he repeated again and again, sobbing —until two strong arms gripped him from behind and lifted him away.

12

THE battle on the mountain was over. They were still fighting at the front and burning one another to ashes around Berlin. But peace had come to the men on the mountain. The ice fortifications were never used.

Mr. All-in-One and a small group of commandos had gone after Chris. In spite of their training and routine, Chris had left them behind. He had dived down impossible slopes where they had had to zigzag. It had irritated them. That puppy, that Colt!

They had cursed him to high heaven but never let him know. They did not tell him that it was wrong to kill the Germans who had come to fetch their dead. In a way, the enemy were at fault. They had a sled full of explosives with them. There was no doubt that they meant to demolish what was left of the camp. Chris's aim had been good.

"He who diggeth a pit . . ." said Mr. All-in-One.

He said nothing to Chris for a long time, and Chris spoke to no one. He no longer knew anyone.

They had had to silence him there by his brother's side in

112

the ruins of the hut. They had to tie him to the ski sled on the way back. He regained consciousness in a bed. He felt cold and spiteful. He remembered everything and hated even his friends.

Mr. All-in-One was there. "Chris," he ventured hesitantly, "it's all over now."

Chris looked at him. "Did they all die?" he asked.

"Yes, they all died."

"Where is Bent?"

"With the others."

Chris said no more. He got up to listen to the news with burning eyes as the speaker continued impersonally.

The end was near. The attack on Berlin had reached the Reichstag building.

Chris laughed when he heard the broadcast. "When do we go into action?"

Bas said, "Let's take a walk, Chris."

There was a full moon. Langestoel looked like some fairy castle.

"You don't understand," said Bas. "Survival is all that matters now."

The conversation ended abruptly. Chris ran inside.

On May 1, the German radio announced that Hitler had committed suicide. Admiral Doenitz had succeeded him. Mussolini had suffered a shameful death. The battle of Berlin was drawing to an end. The first of the freed concentration camp prisoners had crossed the Danish border in the Swedish Count Bernadotte's white busses—the truth about the horrors of the German death camps was known. On Friday, May 4, Field Marshall Montgomery proclaimed that

113

the enemy forces in Holland, northwestern Germany, and Denmark had surrendered. They had yet to surrender in Norway.

The sun shone warmly. It melted away the shields of ice around the machine-gun nests.

Chris met Mr. All-in-One. "Why don't we get moving?"

"Because we are waiting for orders."

The order came through that evening. They were to get back to town and help with law and order. That was all. They started at dawn. Behind them lay the imposing fortress that had never been used. They passed by the charred ruins of Nordseter. All the dead Germans were gone. They headed for the town.

It was a long trip. They passed several blackened ruins. In their helpless fury, the Germans had burned down farms, and when they could not find the saboteurs, they punished everyone. It was the loser's revenge.

Here and there, farmers rummaged disconsolately in the ruins. Sometimes they shook their fists at the soldiers, who now wore the brown uniforms with the Norwegian flag on the right sleeve. Chris understood their anger, even though it was ill-directed. How many of them could say with a good conscience that they had not profited from the situation? That they had not sold eggs and bacon on the black market —possibly even to the enemy—for a high price? Further-more, the traitor who had led the Alpine troops along secret trails to the ambush must be one of them. Their clenched fists did not bother him.

In the valley a fjord boat decked brightly with Norwegian flags waited. There were throngs of people on the quay.

114

They sang and danced. They embraced the soldiers, hugged and kissed them. Someone began singing the national anthem, and soon *Ja, vi elsker dette landet*—"Yes, we love this land"—swelled up to the deep blue spring sky.

It was a glorious moment, and Chris felt a lump in his throat. He didn't know whether or not to feel embarrassed until he saw the tears rolling freely down Mr. All-in-One's cheeks. There were no Germans in sight but many young men with weapons and armbands in Norwegian colors. They walked around keeping an order of sorts but were as overjoyed as all the others.

The boat had steamed up and was ready to sail. The crowd cheered as they cast off. The trip was splendid. The valleys were gay with Norwegian flags; crowds thronged at every landing; there was rejoicing everywhere.

The men passed the time aboard by polishing their weapons. They could still very well get into a fight. The harbor was full of German ships. The Sparks came in with a message, saying that the German flag at the top of the fortress had not yet been taken down.

The commander in chief of the entire Panther Operation addressed them shortly before they sailed into the town. Chris had not seen him before. Tall, tanned, and soft-spoken, he must have been in his middle thirties.

"Our efforts have been rewarded," he said. "Norway is free once more, and our hearts are full of gratitude to those who fell in the struggle.

"The enemy is to be disarmed by Allied and Norwegian forces, and soon we shall be in full control of our country. But remember, surrender does not mean peace. The enemy is still armed. In spite of our rejoicing, it is absolutely necessary to maintain order, dignity, and discipline."

The speech was heard in silence, but later several of the soldiers grumbled. Hadn't they maintained order and dignity long enough?

The commander listened in disapproval. He began to speak once more. "Provocative conduct toward the defeated enemy will not be tolerated. Any attempt to take the law into your own hands will be severely dealt with. Don't forget that!"

No one said anything, but the expression on Chris's face told all. Mr. All-in-One walked up, smiling.

"You didn't like that, did you?"

"We have to treat the murderers like tourists, of course."

"We have to treat them according to the law."

"What do they know about the law?"

"It's time they learned."

"Not with my help, they won't."

Mr. All-in-One looked at him with concern. "Chris, what do you think you'll do now?"

Chris said, "I don't think!"

This was not true. He thought a great deal. Mr. All-in-One was worried. "Don't ever be afraid to have feelings," he said and left.

Chris looked after him scornfully. They had just been told that feelings were not allowed. Mr. All-in-One was a nincompoop.

There were no incidents as they sailed into the town harbor. They passed directly under the fortress where the Swastika still waved, and the guards were at their posts.

"The fools," Chris thought.

Nothing happened.

Chris had never seen the town so beautiful. The birch trees had fresh green leaves, and the mountainside was covered with bright foliage. The red, white, and blue flags were everywhere. There was a tremendous crowd at the pier. Cheers rained down on them. They were the first Free Norwegian troops to reach the town, and the people were going wild. Everyone wanted to shake their hands, to kiss them, and to slap them on the back.

The commander was firm. The enemy stood ready with loaded guns a mere hundred meters away, waiting for someone to whom they could surrender.

"Ready, march!"

It was a march of triumph, but Chris was sorry there were no Germans on the street.

They were quartered in his old school. Strutting around the empty classrooms should have been fun; instead he felt disgusted. The place smelled musty. It smelled of sweat and of humiliation. The school had been nothing but a necessary evil to him before, and now the old-fashioned rooms and the corridors with their rows of pegs filled him with an unutterable hatred.

He was to sleep in the physics lab. He unrolled his blanket and marked it with his name. Then he went out into the yard where he had played ball, teased the girls, and furtively done his homework.

At least the yard had been fun, but it meant nothing to him now. He knew he would never go back to school.

He felt a strange loneliness. The others had been sent out

117

on patrol duty or were posted as guards. When he asked Bas for something to do, he was told to take it easy. Besides, there would be some excitement soon. And there was.

A truck suddenly lurched to a stop in front of the iron gate that he had hurried through so often when the school bell rang. Soldiers with machine guns stood in the back of the truck, and a group of men and women sat huddled in the middle with their hands over their heads. Someone shouted, "Traitors," and in a moment the truck was surrounded by a mob that spat and swore at the prisoners. It was disgusting to see, but, strangely, Chris enjoyed it.

The prisoners were herded down from the truck and led single file into the gym.

More trucks pulled up in quick succession, and the crowd that gathered almost stopped the traffic.

The prisoners were a sorry-looking bunch: weeping young women with shaven heads who had been friendly with the Germans; distinguished-looking gentlemen loudly calling upon the Geneva Convention. Collaborators! Then there were the smart young blades with smooth smiles—the opportunists. They, too, were poked in the back with Sten guns.

Chris sickened at the sight of them. He walked away. The town looked as if everyone in it were at one huge party. People clung to him to show their gratitude. It made him feel both proud and angry. To his relief, bagpipes were heard from the harbor.

The first Allied troops had arrived.

Crowds descended upon them, but they marched on steadily, quite unaffected by all the excitement. Chris had never seen anything like it. That was the kind of soldier he wanted to be, steady and unruffled; that was the kind of man he wanted to be.

He walked back to the school. There was something he wanted to talk to Bas about. A crowd of people still lingered around the iron gate. They whistled through their fingers and howled each time a prisoner was brought in. "Those fools," Chris thought. They had done nothing to resist the injustice and the disgrace. He was standing looking at them with contempt when Mr. All-in-One walked up and gave him a friendly kick on the shin.

"How do you feel now?"

Chris did not reply.

"Bas would like to talk to you."

"I was just on my way to him."

They walked across the yard without speaking. Bas had established himself in the teachers' room. Chris had only been there a couple of times before when he had had to account for some trouble he had been in. The room had always been thick with tobacco smoke. He did not like the teachers' room.

Everything was different now. Bas sat at the headmaster's table, the throne from which the headmaster had always spoken of respect for one's superiors. His own father had sat at that same table. Chris had never been able to understand it. In many ways his father had been an indulgent man.

The room was changed with Bas there. The tobacco smoke was there but no uneasiness. It was no longer a frightening room to enter. Bas was tired, his eyes were closed, but he looked at peace with himself.

119

"Colt, my friend, are you pleased?"

Chris shook his head. "When will they bring Bent here?" he said.

"Tomorrow or perhaps the day after."

The question seemed to surprise Bas. He added, "He will be buried with military honors, with the others."

Chris shrugged his shoulders. The funeral didn't interest him. It was the grave that mattered.

Bas said, "Are you all alone now?"

Chris nodded. Why all this talk about nothing! "Who betrayed Bent and the others?" he asked.

"Chris," Mr. All-in-One began, but Bas interrupted him.

"You have a right to know what we know," he said, "but first you must realize that all is still confusion. We know nothing definite about the luckless action, and I doubt that we will ever know the full truth. All of them lost their lives." Bas added, "The boat group was liquidated before they ever reached land, and the land group had no survivors, either. Your brother was the only survivor from the sabotage group —and then Tom, who arrived too late."

"And Tom is dead," Chris blurted out.

"We suspected Tom as little as we suspected your brother," said Bas.

"But who was the traitor?"

"Paul."

"Who is Paul?"

"He was the leader of the land group."

"I don't understand." Chris was puzzled.

Bas said, "To understand, you must know more of the background. The Germans had two systems of espionage.

120

Sipo and *Abwehr*. The Gestapo was part of the *Sipo*—short for *Sicherheits Politzei*—while the *Abwehr* concerned itself with active espionage and counter-espionage. There was some rivalry between these two groups. Paul was one of *Sipo*'s agents. London thought he was a patriot, so he was able to pass on a great deal of vital information to the enemy. The bombing of the submarine base was staged to strike a decisive blow at the underground. Three groups were to take part in the action and to be wiped out! The time difference and the moving of the lighted markers was sheer genius, all the doing of the Gestapo.

"The guarding of the oil tanks on the promontory was the *Wehrmacht's* and the *Abwehr's* job. We do not know why the *Abwehr* knew nothing of the action that was to take place on the promontory. Paul must have felt sure that this land group would quickly be surrounded by overwhelming numbers and be forced to surrender. When this did not happen, we must assume he used the delayed bomber attack as an excuse to try to call off the action. The only logical conclusion is that the boys in the group refused and attacked regardless, with the results we now know. The sabotage group had time to blow up the oil tanks, and Paul got what was coming to him."

Chris had listened to the explanation keenly. "But why did the Gestapo come to our house?"

"The Gestapo paid everyone a visit just in case any of them should survive."

"The Gestapo did not come to Tom's place, and Tom was late. Doesn't that seem suspicious?"

Bas looked at him for a long time with sad eyes. "No."

121

"Why not?"

"Because Paul was Tom's brother."

That was the end of the conversation. Bas said he hoped Chris would stay with them for a while, and Chris answered that he probably would.

Mr. All-in-One suggested that Chris should go home to see how things were. Chris agreed, although he had no desire to do so.

He walked out into the jubilant town with his head full of conflicting thoughts.

Chris almost wished he were not in uniform the way people fell over him. The women were syrupy. "Aren't you young to be a soldier? . . . Our young hero!" He shrugged off their hugs and their kisses.

It was a long way home. He tried to get on the streetcar. There were flags in front and flags behind. The passengers stood packed together. They even stood on the steps and called to him when the car stopped. "Jump aboard, soldier!"

He was not about to. He wanted to stay away from their hands and their praise.

He walked over to the railway station. He would use Bent's tunnel. He felt that he was going to relive something. How long had he been away? Not even three weeks. The sky had been an inferno that evening he had met Bent at the mouth of the tunnel. Now he could safely walk up to it. That was one difference.

There was still another difference—inside himself. He felt it, but he didn't understand it.

There was a crowd at the station. People stood in groups and talked excitedly. Something was going on. They stepped aside to let him through.

122

"Make way for the soldier."

He stood there and did not know where to go. Military policemen with white sticks were lined up along the platform.

"Where to?"

He was free to go wherever he pleased.

"What's going on?" Chris asked.

"We're waiting for prisoners released from the concentration camps," was the answer, "the very first ones to be released."

He walked into the station. Ambulances were parked along the platforms. Chris was uncomfortable. The atmosphere under the shattered glass domes and rusty steel girders was uneasy and tense.

"Where are they coming from?" asked Chris.

"From Hell," answered a Red Cross nurse.

Another nurse added, "Only the ones in the best shape are coming back."

Chris looked at her, puzzled. "What do you mean?"

The nurse looked doubtful. He was so young. She said quietly, "Not all of them had the strength to survive the peace."

The train pulled in slowly. She continued, "The rest will be buried. Our people will have to do it. And the Americans and the Russians. The Germans will just sit around and act shocked. They are false—a plague."

Chris had never looked at it like this before. To him the Germans had simply been the enemy. With better weapons they could be defeated. This was different. The war not only meant the dead but also the crippled and the maimed.

The train drew to a noisy stop.

Some passengers leaned out of the window. They looked as if their bodies had shrunk ridiculously inside their clothes and their faces had become shadows.

Then they climbed out of the train. Some fell because their legs could not carry them. Chris knew that he would not forget this pitiful sight as long as he lived. Most of the prisoners were carried out on stretchers.

Chris walked around the stretchers and down the tracks toward the tunnel and on through it.

He stood at the mouth of the tunnel where Bent had wiped the blood off his face. He stood there below the hill, with the house perched on top like a fortress. That house belonged to him. His room was there with all his things in it. Bent's things and his father's were there as well. He felt revengeful. The house on the hillside should be burned—burned to ashes. It would make a gigantic bonfire. That would end his childhood.

The neighbor boy saw him under the tree.

"Why, Chris—and in uniform, too! Come home with me!"

"No."

"Why not?" He would not be put off. So Chris went.

They celebrated his return. Chris liked them. They meant well.

"*Skoal,* Chris!" They drank to his health.

They begged him to tell where he had been. Not far. What had he been doing? Nothing much. What was he going to do now? Well, he thought of staying in the army a while. Was he hungry? No, thanks. He had to go take a look at the house.

Someone asked about Bent.

Chris stood up. "I must go," he said.

Would he like them to go with him? No, thanks.

The lights were on in the house, and he heard voices and laughter. The door was open, and he walked in hesitantly. There were people in the living room, and the phonograph was scratching out:

> "Now forever
> And forever
> I love you . . ."

He wrenched open the door to the living room.

"What in hell is going on here?"

There were three people in the room: a woman in the arms of a British soldier in the dark corner by the bookshelf and a large red-faced man in his shirt sleeves. The table was full of bottles and glasses, and the man in shirt sleeves took an unsteady step in his direction.

"What the devil," he began, but then he opened his arms expansively.

"A soldier," he snuffled. "Welcome to our home!" He was about to embrace Chris, who sidestepped out of his reach.

"Who are you?" demanded Chris. He tried to make his voice sound cold, but it trembled.

"Hansen. Carpenter Hansen!"

The stranger was bursting with good will. He fumbled for a glass and a bottle.

"Come and have a drink. It's the real thing!" He pointed at the soldier, who was too drunk to respond. "A gift from our friend here, straight from the kingdom of England. We're lucky, eh!"

125

Chris refused the glass. "What are you doing here!" It was hard for him to control himself.

"I live here," answered the other, bewildered, "but what are you doing here?"

"I live here," Chris said slowly, emphasizing each word. "This is my house."

The carpenter blinked. "You live here, too?" Suddenly it dawned on him. "Now I know. You are one of those who escaped from the Nazis. Lucky for you we were home. Hey, Englishman, come and meet the host."

The Englishman looked up dully. When he saw Chris, he tried to scramble to his feet, with difficulty. The woman on his lap plopped onto the floor.

The soldier, a Red Devil, saluted.

"Comrade," he gabbled. "Comrade."

Then he fell back limply into the chair.

The carpenter started the phonograph again. *"Blutrote Rosen . . ."* He waltzed around and brought Chris another drink. When Chris refused, he downed it with relish himself.

"What luck I met him." He virtually glistened with pleasure. "What would he have done with all his whiskey and cigarettes. He had a bagful of the stuff. A stranger in a foreign city. We sure have been lucky."

Chris eyed him in disgust. The room smelled of alcohol and cigarette smoke. Ashes were strewn everywhere.

Muffled shouts sounded from the next room, from his own room. He opened the door. Two boys about ten or twelve were amusing themselves by shooting sparrows in the big tree with a sling. He snatched it away from them, slapped them hard across the face, and shoved them out of the room. They both cried for their father. The carpenter

126

came stumbling in. "What are you doing to my boys."

"They have no business in my room."

"It's their room now."

"Not any more, it isn't. They will have to get out! You will all have to get out!"

The carpenter set down his glass. In his fury he might have smashed it.

"Is that so? This is our house now, and you can borrow a couch if you shut up, you snotty brat. We have been quartered here legally. The damned English—excepting Tommy over there, he's all right—blew our house to bits. My wife is still buried under the ruins." He sniffled. "Lucky the boys were with their grandmother when it happened."

"Where were you?"

"In the submarine base, of course, where else?"

"So you worked for the Germans?"

"Shut up with that hogwash! A man has to live. What the hell do you know about life?"

The quarrel had attracted the attention of the Englishman and the woman. They stood swaying in the doorway, looking on. To his horror, Chris recognized her. It was the woman with the scar, the informer.

Shock and anger almost paralyzed him.

"Do you know her?" Chris said in as controlled a voice as he could manage.

The carpenter smiled amiably. "Annie? Of course I know Annie. She's Tommy's girl. Tommy's friends are my friends. Come and say hello to her."

Chris shuddered. He could see she remembered. She looked afraid, but her expression changed to defiance and contempt.

127

If he had had a weapon, he would have shot her.

She stared him down brazenly. He flinched under her scornful gaze.

He slammed the door, crawled out the open window onto the balcony and up the sturdy branch to the tree house over the hill.

It was exactly the way he had left it. Nobody had discovered his secret. Even Bent had not known about it. Now Bent was gone. Chris realized he had never really been close to him or to his father. They had both been strangers to him —just as the house had become an unfamiliar place.

The phonograph started playing once more.

> *"Ich tanze mit dir*
> *in den Himmel hinein . . ."*

The sky was illuminated as it had been on the last evening he had waited here for Bent. People were using all the fireworks they had hidden away for so long. It sounded like a barrage of antiaircraft fire. Bonfires burned in all the streets and up the mountainside. People were burning their blackout curtains.

Chris had no desire to burn the blackout curtains. The fireworks didn't interest him. The house did not matter— these people did not matter.

He remembered Bent's last words there in the board hut, "If you hate, you lose," and he knew he was dangerously close to losing. "Hate kills more of us than war," Mr. All-in-One had said. Chris was beginning to understand what he and Bent had meant. Somehow he must fashion a life for himself from what he had left—that was what mattered. Only then would he have survived the fight.

128